# Twisting Tide

## PAMELA ST ABBS

Twisting Tide © 2010 Pamela St Abbs

ISBN:
ISBN-13: 978-0957403062
ISBN-10: 0957403062
Published by Palmer Books

DEDICATION

For Ross, Willie and Karen

# CONTENTS

# Acknowledgement

With thanks to Bill

Chapter 1

Police cars made Carroll Enderby nervous. Every time she saw one her heart would speed while she would lift her foot from the accelerator. The strength in her normally taught leg muscles would uncontrollably relax making it difficult to use any of the pedals in the car. If only her heart muscle could relax too.

Traffic lights ahead told her to stop. She angled herself so she could see round her sun visor when she got close to them. Slow and steady. Isn't that what she had been taught? She managed to lay her foot on the brake. She shivered. Her earlier trip out of the car had chilled her. November sun gave so little heat, she decided, putting the fan on to blow engine-warmed air into the car.

Waiting now. She looked in her rear-view mirror. The policeman was on his own. His pastel eyes were focussed on hers through the glass. She looked away wondering if she had shown the guilt she felt. She'd been tense this Friday morning when she'd looked at herself in the bathroom mirror and seen her twenty-five year old face looking ridiculously innocent back at her. She'd assessed the hotchpotch of family genes that had given her dark blue eyes and coffee coloured hair. No, there was nothing in her looks that could mark her as a criminal. Her nerves made her yawn and stretch out bending her thin arms inside her jumper beyond the normal allowance for elbows.

The traffic lights changed and she snapped them back so her hands were gripping the steering wheel. She mustn't give the policeman an excuse to stop her. The next set of lights was changing against her. Normally she would have pulled into the outside lane and put her foot down, but she couldn't with him behind her. He was going to make her late.

And Geraldine Franson would be there looking, thinking, judging her. And like an older sister she had unattainable knowledge. She had the same ingredients in her build and her looks as herself but arranged in perfect order. And she had an honest exterior that demanded respect, and she had wealth. Carroll wanted to be like her, but she knew she never could and she hated Geraldine for it.

Green. The police car was still following her. The laboratory was all the way through the other side of town. Normally she would have used the by-pass to get to work except for the out of town visit she'd made earlier, before heading towards St John's Town for work.

Perhaps he was following her because of that stop she'd made. But she didn't think that the police got involved in that sort of thing and she dared not even think about it now. She hadn't parked where she shouldn't. She was always careful.

Red. Every traffic light seemed to be against her. She stopped and started each time with supreme care. She tried not to look, but she couldn't help it and every time his cool eyes looked back. What was she doing wrong? She couldn't think. Her brake lights and indicators were okay; they'd been checked last weekend.

The yellow and chocolate coloured bricks of St John's Town gave way to the wider roads of the outer villages which had long since merged together to form the main area of housing for the town. The policeman was still following. Perhaps she was being too careful. She pushed the accelerator a little more, she would try driving a little faster. Hadn't she been told once that the police went for people who were sticking too closely to the speed limit?

The last set of traffic lights and she would be heading towards the countryside – and he still hadn't stopped her. What was he waiting for? What did he want?

Perhaps she did look a little young with her tiny build and round face, but lots of people her age had company cars.

Carroll looked at the woodland she was driving through. It was quiet, but there were cars drawn up on the sandy grass verge while their owners walked dogs. It wouldn't be so bad being stopped here.

She turned left down a narrow road which took her downhill and out of the woodland. A vast expanse of flat green fields lay far ahead of her. Occasional hedges made grey lines and ditches made sky-blue bands, which criss-crossed each other like a game-board. She checked. Yes, he was still following.

Her destination stood beyond the fields, closer to the sea than the new suspension bridge. The laboratory straddled between river mouth and land on stilts. She thought it looked like a dead spider, stiff and straight legged. And Stranfield, her boss, was like the spider poised on the edge of its web ready for the kill. Perhaps the policeman was going to the laboratory too. They just happened to be going in the same direction. Her relief allowed her to remember,

'Of course,' she said, her deep scratchy voice catching at the words, 'Geraldine won't be there. She's on holiday for three whole weeks.' She smiled: being Friday meant Geraldine was one week down with two to go. In her absence Carroll would be going on a course on Monday – Geraldine had booked it. And next Saturday she was due to walk out on the wash to collect the cockles and muscles instead of Geraldine.

Then she looked in her mirror. The police car was edging out to pass her. There were no cars parked down this road, no houses, no people. Carroll didn't want to be stopped here.

There was barely enough room for two cars. Her inside wheels jagged on the verge as she tried to give him enough room. They jerked at her steering wheel throwing her off balance.

A sign lit up in his back window, "police stop."

Carroll tried to stop slowly and steadily but somehow missed the clutch, or scrambled the gears – she wasn't sure which – and her car slewed to a halt. A strand of her fringeless bob fell across her eyes. She poked it out of the way as the policeman sidled his tall, broad shouldered body around to her window. He tapped on it so she wound it down. He tilted his hat up displaying a curly, blonde stubble of hair. Squatting down he smiled at her.

'You were going a little over the speed limit in town,' he said.

'Was I?' said Carroll. Her voice broke the words as it always did when she was scared. 'I'm sorry. I didn't mean to.' Her mind raced for an excuse for her strange behaviour, but none came. She looked at his pale green eyes and the pale lashes around them and made her mouth smile. She judged that he couldn't be that much older than her. Perhaps that was it. She could almost see the testosterone circulating in his blood stream. She knew he'd done it for a buzz. It had just been a power game to him, made more delicious to his glands by her being female. He'd stopped her because he could. And she was almost too relieved to care.

He asked for the car's number and her papers. The first she gave without difficulty, the second she did not have on her.

'This time I'll let it go,' he said writing out a white form. 'But you'll have to present your documents at the Police Station within the week.'

Chapter 2

Curran Elves heard the timbers of his boat, Lara Lynn, groan at the loss of the Wash waters supporting her hull. His mug of tea warmed his reddened hands as he readied his thick set body for the work to be done on the sand bank. He put his mug down next to the radio set, chucked his mussel baskets over the side and followed them onto the soft sandy mud left by the retreating tide.

In the distance the dark grey bodies of seals flopped into the water. Curran looked towards St John's Town – its skyline still visible across the sand, water, mud and marsh grass of the Wash, and then the river. The new suspension bridge dwarfed the church's spire, corn silos and dock cranes that jabbed at the sky like needles. Nearer, but still on the other side of the river he could see the white square of the laboratory built so it could draw sea water straight from the Wash. He always felt that the two dark squares of window were looking at him. He turned away to gather his mussels.

He didn't like the idea of the laboratory. It wasn't there for conservation, or to prevent pollution. He knew that. It was run by some small high tech firm. He'd seen the fancy car its boss, Stranfield, drove. His name was in the newspaper every week donating money or doing some good work. Why should anyone try that hard? People like that crazed you.

Turning his thirty year old weathered face to the sandy mud of Catstail Sand Bank he started to gather the mussels which formed small black mounds over the sand bank. He didn't hold with the modern method of sucking them up when the tide was over them, like many fishermen harvested cockles.

Harvesting mussels made him sweat. But there was a freedom out here he no longer had at home.

'Lara Lynn,' he said. Was there any luck to be had in naming your boat after your wife when your wife no longer loved you, he wondered. He'd wanted a wife and children in spite of or, perhaps, because of Gran

Charlotte's warnings against them. And now he didn't want to say she was right.

He stood up to stretch his back. He was wary of the fine blue sky and even of the sea retreating behind him. The fisherman's blood that coursed through his veins told him something was wrong. He couldn't see it, hear it or smell it, but he knew better than to trust such outward signs of safety. He knew how quickly the weather could change. From calm the wind could surge and turn the sea into a powerful force that could crush a boat. And fog could take your sight away just when home was on the horizon.

Hadn't he seen a holy man standing on the sea wall as the Lara Lynn had made her way up the channel this morning? The monk's brown robes had wrapped around bare legs and the cowl had been pushed back showing a high shining dome and a solid hawk face. Every fisherman knew the sight of a holy man meant trouble as surely as a hole in the hull of his boat.

A gull dipped level with Curran's eye line. It flew close to his face before skewering up and away. He swung his fist at the bird and swore at it.

He stopped. Further along the sand bank he saw a crop of black mussels growing in a large mound exposed by the retreating waters. The seaweed they were clinging to glistened white in the sun. The shimmer of water on the sand bank looked like the sky, but Curran knew it wouldn't be like walking on clouds. His weight would push him into the mud which seemed to get softer and more difficult to walk on as the tide went out. But he would get them anyway. He could do with a good catch.

As he walked he was caught by the roar of a jet plane lining up for the bombing range on sand banks beyond this one. The scream of its engines made him duck and cover his ears in pain. He saw the pilot in the cockpit and then the aircraft was gone. He was closer to what he'd thought to be a large mussel bed, and the dark and light areas became clearer. It looked like bits of loose black plastic wrapping ripped and flapping around a white log. It had the familiar sound of his wife's clean sheets on the washing line. He slowed and wondered if it was worth his while to finish the journey and take a look. But he'd heard all sorts of stories about people finding valuables washed up, so he thought he would.

Curran didn't see what it was straight away. But when he touched it the texture of soft wet flesh made him jump back. Part of him didn't want to look, but some ghoulish curiosity made him look again. He could tell it was a woman. He could see her silken evening dress. But all was in shreds. Her body was a mess of deep cuts. Worst of all he couldn't find her face, only some dark brown hair. The body moved settling itself down now its bed of water had gone.

He ran. His fishing boots smacked against his legs as he dragged his feet out of the sucking mud. Before him all he could see was Lara's face. His wife's scraggy black hair was so similar to his own. Her tiny features and broad cheek bones and small frame were like a pixie's. It was for a moment as if it was his wife lying there. Part of him felt sick, another part of him wished it was her, but he knew it was not. She would be with those monks cleaning and scrubbing for them. This was her fault. She sent the monk out to the sea wall. She brought this on him.

His eyes cleared. His boat lay before him like a beached whale. His heart and lungs hurt inside his chest. Back on the Lara Lynn he clutched the hand set of his radio.

'Lara Lynn to St John's Town Coast Guard. Over.'

'St John's Town Coast Guard. Over,' the radio crackled back to him. He wiped the salty water from his face and pretended it was sea spray as his exhausted limbs trembled. When he spoke again he had to hold his voice so tightly he could barely tell them what he'd seen.


'Thank you, DC Garden, DC Flagg,' Campbell dismissed them, his Edinburgh accent making his gratitude sound generous.

'Sir,' said DC Lawrence Flagg. His body was held stiffly, and, Campbell noted, his green eyes avoided looking at his own. Flagg's body tilted forward slightly making his height and wide shoulders tower over Campbell as if he was trying to be intimidating. His knew sports jacket and crisp shirt made Campbell feel slightly shabby. They were as new as Flagg was to the job, Campbell reminded himself while blowing his nose.

He watched DC Sally Garden's fuzzy pony tail and Flagg's spiky fair hair as they left his office. It seemed strange to see Garden out of uniform and he wondered if she would cope with the change of work. He turned away and reached for the coat peg. It had been a long week; a lunch at home was just what he needed.

While he placed his spidery arms in his ancient great-coat he watched the chaos of the Ouse Crossing market stalls below him. The order of the office had been upon him for weeks. The house was decorated and Margaret wouldn't let him start on the garden pond until next spring.

As he went for his car his great-coat weighed across his bony shoulders like the lack of activity weighed on his mind. Thus he'd found Sergeant

Parnold seconded to the Met. And, DC Bridget Jenner taking the opportunity to go on a course. At least the equal viciousness of the wind and the sun were a relief.

Such a large coat was a nuisance in the car and his Remembrance poppy was loose. He removed the paper flower and fixed it to his jacket. Then he folded the steel grey fabric of his coat and laid it on the back seat. He looked at his controls. Twenty five years of driving had left them as alien to him as the first time he'd seen them. He partly blamed his childhood spent mostly on foot or on public transport in Edinburgh, but few could avoid using a car in East Anglia.

He joined the traffic with a grunt. The car steamed up. He turned on the fan. Fumes from the other cars and lorries flooded through the vents so he turned the fan off. Taking the back road he was soon beyond the land set aside for industry. The dark man-made pine forest of the chalk-lands briefly stretched out below him before the road plunged among it. He seemed a long way from the low lying flat fields of the fens here. And yet, he knew, beyond the rolling slopes the land fell away into that huge basin of silt and black soil which collected the water from the surrounding higher ground and funnelled it out to the sea.

Several miles on the forest cleared on the far side of the road and a right hand turning was sign posted. He took it. High neatly clipped hedges surrounded him, and blue gates flicked past his window.

Everywhere there were reminders of past cases. They had been resolved, but he didn't look upon them as triumphs. There had been too many deaths along the way. He had gone over them so often in his mind and knew he could not have done more, but he could not shake off a feeling of responsibility.

He knew he was pondering these things due to a lack of activity – and for that he should be grateful. It meant that there was orderly life going on around him, no murder anyway.

But the approaching winter was taking life slowly from the fields and Campbell felt he had to keep himself from decaying like last summer's bracken so he searched for signs of the long distant spring. He noted the lakes of plastic, covering carrot seed, and sprigs of winter wheat pushing up among the light soil of the chalk lands.

Having just settled himself to the task of getting home in one piece a tractor with bloated tyres on to keep it sinking into the autumn mud pulled out of a gateway near a junction. Swerving to avoid it put him on the road that took him through the village instead of his usual short cut down a narrow lane to his cottage.

The long slope up the village made the square Norman tower of the church seem even higher than it really was against the mostly modern houses, Victorian school and cheaply built post-war village hall. The smells of burnt sugar caught in his nostrils and he smiled, the last reminder of the growing seasons, the factory processing the beet into sugar.

He waggled his neck from side to side to loosen it. He felt he must be getting a cold. The low winter sun flicked through the trees and buildings casting long shadows then bright splashes of light despite being the middle of the day. He couldn't cope with the glare so he reached for his sun glasses and was caught by a sneeze. When he looked again at the road it was blocked by a woman in her twenties in jeans and a green wax jacket. She was waving her arms about.

Swerving slightly to miss her plump frame, he stopped.

'Quick,' was all she managed to say at him. Her pink and white face pleaded some sort of urgency she couldn't put into words. He allowed her to pull him from the car. A baby squalled from the pram parked on the pavement and a dog jiffled its bottom as it tried to wag its tail while remaining seated.

'Here. Smoke… Fumes,' said the young woman. 'Everyone's out. I can't find anyone to help.' Her voice was raised to a near scream as she finished and she clutched her mouth.

He followed her down the short drive of a modern brick bungalow with her tugging at his sleeve. He guessed that because of his unmarked car she hadn't realised he was a policeman. She pointed at the garage.

'I can't open it,' she said.

The familiar smell of exhaust fumes filled his nostrils. 'Get an ambulance,' said Campbell. 'Have you got a mobile phone?'

'Not on me,' said the woman.

Seeing that she was thinking about the distance to the phone box, her baby and her dog and these thoughts were jamming up her ability to help he tried to shove her into action with a Scottish, 'What's your name?'

'Polly.'

'Polly, here's mine.' He handed her his mobile. 'Hurry now. I'm a policeman.'

It worked. As she left him and stood by her dog and pram to make the phone call, he checked the up and over garage door and knew even the crow-bar in his car would not shift it. He looked along the side of the building. A side door.

'It's locked,' called the young woman from the pavement.

Taking the crow bar from the boot he could just see the top of her blond hair and hear her call herself Polly Browme on the radio to his base.

His reserve of energy was unusually large due to the limited routine forced on him in the last few weeks and due to his cold not really getting hold of him yet. But no matter how fast he ran he wanted to move quicker. Even jimmying the door seemed to take minutes instead of the reality of seconds before the wood around the lock split with a crack.

Holding his breath he hurried across the garage to the car and reached over a prone man covering the two front seats to turn off the engine. The deathly throb of the motor stopped.

Allowing his hand to fall from the key Campbell found his head next to the man's chest. A clean shaven chin almost touched his own dark hair when the man's head rolled sideways. A strand of malt and white coloured hair fell from where the thick locks had been dressed away from his face. It touched Campbell's hand which he'd placed on the back of the seat to balance himself.

Inside the muscled chest he could hear the flutter of a heartbeat. Unexpectedly Campbell found himself pleading inside, 'Don't die. Please don't die.' As he pulled the man out of the car he heard a clatter of something being dragged out by the man's foot. He didn't stop to see what it was, he knew he had to get this man out of the garage quickly.

The casualty's large bone structure and athletic build made Campbell's load heavy. His own lungs clutched at his throat demanding air. He denied them until he stumbled through the side exit knocking the key from the inside of the dangling lock.

Crumpled against the door post Campbell gasped, coughed and wiped his smarting eyes. Looking up he saw Polly Browme's sturdy legs spread to help take the unconscious man's weight. The air was still mixed with fumes here so Campbell nodded and they carried him out to the front to wait for the ambulance.

He stooped over his patient to look for chest movements. He loosened his shirt and checked that his mouth was clear. Laying him on his side he looked at the face of a man who must have seen at least seventy years and wondered at him taking his life in this way. Suddenly, the rush of pleasure he'd got from saving a life began to dwindle. Perhaps this man had a terminal illness and all he'd given him was a more painful end.

The policeman in him told him he would have to find out about him, but somehow nosing about in this man's affairs seemed invasive. Still, he felt the loose tweed jacket pockets and found a Canadian passport. The picture inside told him the man at his feet was Jack Wren. Campbell looked up.

A siren at the far end of the village warned him the ambulance would be here any minute. He bent down to check his patient. He was still breathing, just. He watched the grey face for signs of movement until the ambulance crew arrived and nudged Campbell out of the way. Fixing an oxygen mask over Jack Wren's face they took him into the care of their stiff white-boxed ambulance.

Polly Browme had lifted her baby from the pram, swathed it in crocheted blankets and was rocking it to and fro. Campbell thought she might be trying to comfort herself more than it.

'Do you know him?' asked Campbell nodding at the back of the ambulance.

'Not really.' Campbell noted her accent wasn't totally local. There was a hint of Queen's English which he associated with Sussex. 'I've seen him in the village off and on for the last few weeks,' she continued. 'He turned up shortly after Georgina Brightwood died. She used to live here with her daughter, Agatha Spier. I haven't seen Mrs Spier for about a week. Someone said she'd gone to Africa on business.'

'Does anyone else live here?'

'Not as far as I know. Mr Spier died several years ago now, and Agatha Spier has a daughter, but I don't know where she lives. I'm from further up the hill. I was only taking a walk.'

She was looking in need of her own home and a cup of tea so Campbell put her address in his note book and allowed her to go. As he did so he recalled the clatter he'd heard in the garage as he'd drawn Jack Wren out of the fumes. It hadn't sounded like a seat-belt buckle so he put on a polythene glove and took a couple of deep breaths and braced himself for the return to the now thinning exhaust gasses.

He held his breath and felt along the garage floor near the open car door. Even through his glove, his knuckles were scuffed by concrete until they made contact with a smooth hard box. As he picked it up his fingers curled into velvet held stiffly into a moulded shape. Tucking the box into his pocket he felt again and found a pair of tweezers. Back out in the air he popped the two items into plastic bags and labelled them with the time, date, address and the name Jack Wren.

When he returned to his car he chucked them in the boot without giving them any more thought as he could hear the radio calling him.

He let the information he received sink in. He was wanted in St John's Town at the harbour where a boat was waiting for him. He knew the journey would take half an hour from here and there would be a limit on the details he would be told over the radio. This vacuum caused his body to tense underneath his rounded shoulders, and his throat to feel dry and sore. His mind was already primed for an investigation and he was relieved not to have to consider what he'd done to Jack Wren.

Chapter 3

Inside the small cabin of the sea-fisheries boat Campbell pulled on his green rubber boots over his thick socks. He arranged the yellow waterproof trousers, he'd been loaned, outside his boots so that any water would not run in and wet his feet. He pressed cotton wool into his ears and covered them, and his short dark hair, with his wool hat as instructed by his guide to help prevent the thrumming of the wind giving him a head-ache. The rustle of his waterproof jacket and trousers seemed to travel up his ears internally as he made his way up on deck where a dinghy was being lowered into the Wash by their guide, Harry Blacking.

The police doctor, Doctor Hok, and DC Garden, dressed similarly to Campbell, looked round at him. Both the soft flesh of the policewoman's and the golden skin of the doctor's face were screwed up against the sun and wind. Next to them two policemen from St John's Town station fiddled with bulging back packs and looked at the water with closed expressions.

Seated in front of the others Campbell examined the curve of water at the bow as the dinghy moved out of the main channel. He was pleased that the activity and the cold wind seemed to have temporarily cleared his cold. Ahead of him he could see several sandbanks. He knew they were spread out for miles in the Wash when the tide was low. In front of Catstail Sandbank, where a fishing boat was beached, Harry Blacking killed the rear-mounted engines and lifted the propellers from the sea, making the rubber dinghy wallow.

Campbell joined the two policemen from St John's Town, Garden and Doctor Hok in the shallows and found himself up to his knees in cold brackish water. Behind him he heard the splash of Harry Blacking slipping into the Wash so that between them they could haul the dinghy onto the sand bank.

'Tide's runnin' in now,' said Harry Blacking in a broad local accent.

'You've an hour at most.'

The boots and water-proofs dragged at Campbell as he made his way over the sticky mud. The corrugations left by the sea folded beneath his feet and most of his steps sunk in up to the treads of his boots, and some covered his feet completely. Campbell wondered whether all this sandy mud could really be covered in an hour by the sea.

He covered his ears against the scream of an American jet above him. The noise pushed out all thoughts from his head. A moment later a thud moved through the mud beneath his feet.

'Bombing range,' explained the guide pointing to a sandbank on the horizon.

Several more thumps throbbed through the ground before Campbell and his party reached the small dark shell-fisherman, Curran Elves, who'd found the deceased. The thickset bandy body stood stiff and angry over the corpse like a stone angel in a churchyard. Campbell stationed Garden next to him. He wanted his story before it became a fisherman's legend to be told in the town's pubs for a pint of beer. When he was about to turn from them he noticed Curran Elves spit into the mud and his lips twist into a sneer. He couldn't hear what was said as the wind took their voices away.

As soon as Campbell saw the body he wished he hadn't. He looked up to see how Harry Blacking had responded and saw him gazing back towards the mainland. Campbell turned. Across the strips of sky reflecting sand, petrol blue sea and brown mud he could see what Harry was watching: on the stone wall built along the river channel stood a tiny figure silhouetted against the sun filled water. Campbell asked for binoculars and was handed a set. Long robes flapped about the figure making the silhouette look like a woman in evening dress, except it seemed too bulky for that. It had to be a man.

'Do you know who he is?' Campbell asked Harry.

Harry Blacking crumpled his lined face. Campbell wondered if it was because he couldn't hear him for the wind or whether his Scottish accent was difficult to follow. A moment later he replied, 'I think he gotta be one of the monks from the old Look Out Tower. They run a not very religious retreat centre.' Blacking curled his lip making Campbell think that he looked as if he had sand in his mouth. He also noticed a little relief on Blacking's face as he spoke about something that took him away from the corpse and the activities of the police doctor.

Beyond the monk the river channel cut a band of blue while a white building on stilts blemished the outline of the green bank on the far shore.

'And what's that?' Campbell asked.

'It's a laboratory of some kind. I don't know exactly what they do but one of their girls comes out with me once a month to collect cockles and mussels.'

'Do many people come out on the sand banks?'

'No, it's too dangerous without a guide. The tides rip up and twist round you.'

'Could the body be the girl you bring out here?'

'Geraldine Franson? Why would she come out here on her own?'

Campbell watched Harry Blacking make himself look down at her.

'It could be.' Harry paused and took a deep breath of cold air. When he was steadier he added, 'Except Geraldine Franson is on holiday for three weeks. Next week the other girl's coming out with me instead and I've never met her.'

Briefly it crossed Campbell's mind that this man could have had something to do with this body. The details would have to be checked on return to the mainland. He didn't have very long and he wanted to soak up every piece of information so he turned back to the corpse.

He and Garden would have to do the best they could with photographs and plastic bags because the tide would not wait for a forensic team and Harry Blacking was already saying it was time to think about going.

Through the camera's viewfinder he saw the remains of a young woman with dark hair. Her dress was shredded black satin bleached in places to green by the sea water. There was still a perfect nail on the remains of one hand. Campbell looked at the pale flesh and knew that even if the sea had not taken her life it had taken most of the evidence of her identity.

Surely nothing else could be gained from looking at this mutilated body? He lowered the camera. And, as if by some silent agreement, Doctor Hok arranged for the remains to be placed in a body bag and the two policemen from St John's Town put together a stretcher.

'The lacerations are probably boat damage done after death,' said Doctor Hok. 'I would say, at a guess, she'd been in the water about a week, but whether she died of drowning I can't say. You'll have to wait for the pathology tests. And whether it was suicide, murder or accident may well be up to you to establish.'

Campbell nodded and wiped his nose. He thought of Jack Wren and why he wanted to take his own life and wondered if this girl had chosen her fate or had it chosen for her.

The wail of a pair of aeroplanes caught his eardrums as he spotted Garden gently taking the fisherman's arm to lead him back to his boat. Curran Elves shook himself free and strutted off across the mud. He would have to make a statement later.

Walking behind the returning party Campbell found the ground even heavier. He looked up from his feet from time to time to see the wader-birds still foraging on the mud as if mankind had never walked or died here. And he guessed that once the tide had been over the sandbank there would be nothing to show that this body or this group of oil-skin clad people had ever been on this sand bank.

Back on the boat Campbell pulled the cotton wool out of his ear and yanked off his boots while listening to Garden telling him about the fisherman, Curran Elves. She told him that his wife, Lara, worked at the monastery and that she was also small and dark, like the dead girl. Campbell felt the sweat from his feet chill and wondered how some-one could make a living collecting shell-fish by hand on his own.

And now Campbell had to see the monk. Would he be able to tell him whether the girl was killed or whether she killed herself? Could he tell him who she was? The monk had certainly watched them collect the body from the sandbank. And Curran Elves had told Garden that a monk had been watching when his vessel, the Lara Lynn, went up the channel that morning.

Having left Garden to get Curran Elves's statement and having arranged for Flagg to check out Harry Blacking, Campbell drove over the workings for the new road being built to join up with the suspension bridge and then he turned up the Old Wash Road. The fields stretched out and around him like a calm ocean. The smell of damp cabbages and brussel sprouts filled the car as he passed land chequered with the green vegetable crops and the light coloured soil of the northern fens. The land here supported plants that would grow late into the autumn and could stand until the spring. They were warming to see in their dark green leaves as if winter had been put on hold. Campbell was struck by the way the soil here still had the look of sea bed sand about it, so unlike the southern fens with their heavy black peat.

Beside the road a squat farmer chopped cabbages from their stalks with a long bladed knife and placed them on a conveyor attached to a tractor. He straightened his short back when Campbell asked him the way to the monastery. He assumed that was the right term for the Old Lookout Tower.

'End of the road – as far as you kin go,' he said in a broad Fen accent.

Campbell looked into his ancient face and thanked him.

There was no sign of the wash for as far as he could see. The road was straight and narrow, barely wide enough for one car and there were few passing places. Campbell had seen landscape like this before coming south. He remembered a day when his father had been working out of Edinburgh towards Stirling and young Raymond had gone with him. The land beyond Grangemouth had been flat and fertile giving forth crops of grain. He did not allow himself thoughts of Scotland. This one had crept past his mental barriers.

Of course there were no hills abutting this estuary like the Ochills standing sentinel against the narrowing edges of the Forth so why he'd allowed himself this fancy he did not know. Or, rather, he did know, but he wasn't going to admit it to himself.

As the road approached the Wash the small number of cottages perched on the edges of fields dwindled until there was only the road, which had settled into uncomfortable waves, and the open fields either side of him. This man-nurtured landscape gave him a strange thrill. Surely if Jack Wren had seen this he would not have tried to take his life?

In the distance a bank edged the skyline which was shot through with pink and yellow from the low sun. He'd travelled further north than he'd thought possible on land. That must be the sea bank. A cluster of stark World War II lookout buildings stood over and behind its base. Others around the coast were windowless and empty, but these still looked as if they could be operational. The large lookout window at the top of the tower was glazed with a single sheet. Campbell began to wonder if he could wangle a view from the top before the winter sun sank below the horizon. He was curious to find out just how much could be seen from up there.

The thought crossed his mind, as he parked his car in the gravel car park by the L-shaped group of buildings, that he hadn't been able to see this tower from the sandbank. He made his way up the steep grassy slope. The wind caught him at the top. Staggering back slightly he tried to hide from himself his disappointment in seeing not the sand and mud of the Wash but more fields and a further bank beyond.

'The Wash is bleeding away from us,' said a deep, powerful voice next to him. 'We happily reclaim the land God gives us, and it is fertile.'

When Campbell looked beside him he saw a man as big as the voice had joined him. His companion's brown robes failed to cover his bare ankles and sandals but his cowl hid his head from inspection as well as the wind.

'I'm Brother Joshua, may I help you?'

'Inspector Campbell, Police.' He showed his card.

'Bait diggers and bird watchers use our car park quite often. They walk over the old sea bank along the new wooden path to the new one and then to the mud flats. But we don't often get policemen. Let me show you to my office.' Brother Joshua galloped down the bank and knocked his cowl down onto his shoulders exposing a bald head neatly curbed by a stubble of shaved hair. 'You are a Scot, Inspector.' He extended a solid arm and open hand towards the door.

'Indeed, and yourself?' Not only could this man work out his accent from three words spoken in the wind but he either expected such a visit or he grasped every moment of life with vigour. Campbell remembered that he'd found other religious people to have the same inner verve which had always eluded him.

'I came up from London about five years ago,' said Brother Joshua.

The office was piled high with papers, books and paper-weights. Campbell thought the bobbled plastic chain hanging by the window-blind looked like a rosary. The familiar plinking of a computer came from an open door on the far side of the small room.

'Brother Michael,' explained Brother Joshua, closing the intervening door.

'I believe you saw some activity out on the Wash today?' asked Campbell, again feeling his cold. This time it thickened his voice so he cleared his throat.

'Ah, the body! That was what it was! It has just fallen together in my mind. I've been listening to the local radio. It was mentioned on there that the sea fisheries boat has brought a woman's body in, just moments ago. God rest her soul.' Joshua offered Campbell a seat. 'They sensationalise the news so it ends up sounding like gossip.'

'You were seen on the river channel wall,' said Campbell, sitting down. The stature of this man was singular but Campbell didn't want to sound committed to this view so he asked, 'or one of your colleagues?'

'There is only Brother Michael and myself.' Brother Joshua stepped across the room and opened the door he'd closed earlier. 'Brother Michael, come and meet Inspector Campbell.'

A click and a whine could be heard beyond the door. Then Brother Michael came in. His body was folded into a wheelchair, but above his poorly muscled torso a bright smiling bearded face greeted Campbell.

'Are there no more of you?' Campbell's Edinburgh tones accentuated his surprise.

'We run residential retreats, Inspector,' said Brother Michael. There was a hint in his steady voice of the local tendency to hang on the first beat of a word and dispatch the rest as quickly as possible.

'Have you run any retreats recently?' asked Campbell.

'Not for over a month, Inspector,' said Brother Joshua. 'We've been down in London for two weeks.'

'Doing what?'

'A theological conference, Inspector,' said Brother Michael. 'Talking about God.'

Two weeks would put them out of the area at the time the young woman was estimated to have entered the sea, Campbell noted. He felt slightly guilty for even considering religious men to be possible murderers. And what reason did he have, after all, to believe that this woman had been murdered?

Even if Brother Joshua was just an onlooker, he couldn't resist continuing the conversation. 'How do you manage retreats with just the two of you?' he asked.

'We only have four guests at a time,' said Brother Michael, 'and we have a mother and daughter help us out. We feel vulnerable out here. We can get to know two people and we can trust them. I don't want any more people around than are absolutely necessary.'

'Are your ladies well?'

'Lara is here in the kitchen,' said Brother Joshua. 'Would you like to see her?'

'Just to reassure myself.'

'A pleasure, Inspector.'

'Before we go, could you tell me whether you saw anything unusual in the last few weeks – before your trip to London and since you've been back?'

'I often walk on the sea bank, Inspector,' said Brother Joshua. 'It is why I live here. It brings me in contact with God. I pray mostly But I confess I did not see anything remarkable. Fishing boats come in and out regularly and bigger ships with grain and timber often enough.'

'And today?' asked Campbell. He tried to clear his throat. His chest felt full of glue and it seemed to be forming inside him. He wanted to cough.

'I stood watching the channel for a while in the morning. It was such a bracing day I went back in the afternoon. There was a lot of activity on the sandbank. I'd taken my binoculars for the birds. I don't usually do that, Inspector. I walked out along the channel wall to get a better look. I realised something awful must have happened and chastised myself for my nosiness. I was so ashamed of myself I wanted to be turned into a pillar of salt.'

Brother Michael laughed. 'Brother Joshua is very Old Testament, Inspector.'

Campbell noted Brother Joshua's look of paternal pride every time Brother Michael spoke, even though there could have only been ten years between them – with Brother Joshua only in his mid-thirties. Campbell turned to the younger monk for clarification. 'What do you mean by "very Old Testament"?'

'He loves all the old stories. Christ is a positive newcomer as far as he's concerned and the gospels are so recent they feel as uncomfortable as new boots to him. I'm a New Testament man myself. Are you religious, Inspector?'

'Not in any tangible way.' Campbell felt himself withdrawing and trying to regroup his questions.

'That doesn't sound very decisive,' said Brother Michael.

'A woman has been found dead on the sandbank,' countered Campbell. 'Have you any idea who she could be or how she got there?' His heart sank as he spoke. He knew the direct questions would get simple negative answers and the monks gave them to him. His desire to find out about the dead girl had pushed out his usual tactful unfolding of each individual's story. To complete his routine questions he took the monk's full names down in his notebook: Joshua Alexander and Michael Ridgeway.

He blew his nose and coughed again. Blasted cold was starting to make his head fuzzy. At least he could check on the fisherman's wife, Lara Elves and her mother.

As Campbell followed Brother Joshua through the outside office door and across the yard he was struck by the thought that the monks were far more religious than he'd expected them to be after Harry Blacking's sarcastic comment on the sandbank. He looked hard at Brother Joshua.

Were Harry Blacking's words spoken in jealousy? The L-shaped buildings were freshly decorated in cream wall paint. Through the windows he could see lined curtains and sturdy solid wood furniture.

Beyond the ramped doorway, in the fitted kitchen Campbell found an eighteen year old girl in a cotton print frock rubbing her hands over her extended stomach. She was looking at a refectory table full at one end of polished brass. She seemed proud of her work and proud of her pregnancy.

'Lara Elves?' he asked trying to hold his cold inside himself.

'I'll leave you to it,' said Brother Joshua already moving out of the kitchen door back into the yard.

'Can I have a word?' asked Campbell.

'You kin hiv several,' said Lara Elves in a broad local accent. She gathered her tiny feet clad in black pumps under her chair and folded her thin frock over her bare legs. Campbell felt cold looking at her.

He explained who he was and why he was there. Her brown eyes stared at him. He looked earnestly back at her but found it almost impossible to keep looking as her gaze was so intense. He pruned the information to the minimum leaving out any hints of times or means of death. When he finished she said,

'I reckon I seen it.'

'What have you seen?'

'Her being put in the water. I was pushing my babies across the bridge in their buggy like I do every morning. I leave them with my mum when I come here. It must be about a week ago now.'

'Brother Joshua and Brother Michael were away.'

'I know, but me and mum still come in. We can bring the babies and we can do the jobs we don't have time for usually.' Her tiny hand started to flick at a lank strand of dark hair that had come adrift from her scraped back ponytail. 'Do you want to hear about the body or not?'

Campbell nodded.

'Just below the bridge there was a boat near the bank, on this side of the river. They bundled a great thing into the water. I couldn't see what it was, but I bet it was her.'

'How many people were in the boat?'

'Two. And there was a car in the car park that they built so you can stop and look at the bridge.'

'Men or women?'

'They looked like men to me.'

28

'Could you be precise about the time and day?'

She thought for a moment. 'Yes, a week ago Monday. It's Wednesday today I'n't it? Eight-thirty am.'

'Why didn't you say something before?'

'I thought they might be fishermen.'

'Casting their nets in the river?'

'No, of course not. I'm not stupid. They don't fish like that around here. I thought they might be dumping something like a dead seal. People get all upset about dead seals. My old man's a fisherman. We can do without all that old squit.'

'Was there anyone in the car?'

'Yes, I think there was.'

'Man or woman?'

'Couldn't say. Whoever it was was too busy fiddling with the radio from the look of it.'

'Do you think you could identify the men in the boat?'

'No, they had their backs to me. But one was right fair and the other was right dark haired – darker'n me. And they was big men. Not as big as Brother Joshua, but bigger'n my old man.'

As he jotted down the details in his note book Campbell took himself away from Lara and coughed in a corner. Afterwards he thought about Curran Elves standing over the corpse. Most men would be taller than the shell-fisherman.

'I don't want none of your old germs,' complained Lara.

'Yes, I'm sorry about the cold.' He put his handkerchief away and came back over to her. 'I would like you to make a formal statement. In the mean time I would like to have a word with your mother. Have you got her name and where she lives?'

'Rita Blacking.'

'Harry Blacking's wife?'

'Yes. What's the matter with that?'

'This afternoon I was out on the sandbank with your husband and your father and they never said a word to each other.'

'They wouldn't,' said Lara.

Suddenly the facial expressions of Harry Blacking and the body gestures of Curran Elves fell into place. They hated each other.

'Why don't they speak?'

'I had Curran's first baby when I was fifteen: not legal -- I know that --

and I'd do the same agin now. Hiving babies is what it's all about, Inspector, don't you think?'

'I had my family much later in life,' said Campbell unable to keep a slight frown from his face.

'You're just like my old dad,' said Lara laughing.

She came into the yard with Campbell to point out the direction of her mother's cottage: the last building in the village built along the river bank before it turned into the estuary and where the old sea bank joined the new sea bank.

'There's no road directly from it to the monastery, and it's about a quarter of a mile walk along the old sea bank,' said Lara Elves.

He looked at the way she pointed and then up at the look-out tower above them. It was three storeys high with slits cut into the bricks about half-way up before the big window.

'Can I see it from there?' he asked.

'Yes,' said Lara Elves.

She took him through a third door in the L-shaped set of buildings. Like all the others from the yard into the monastery, it was served by a ramp. Lara put on a light to show up the steps lining the rectangular tower beyond an entrance hall.

Having had Lara point out the light on the end of her mother's house Campbell took in the darkening sky. But even from this vast glass window the Wash could not be seen as it was hidden by the new sea bank. But Campbell spotted a green line above and beyond the far bank he hadn't noticed before. It looked like another shorter bank built behind the sea defence.

'What's that?' he asked.

'My dad says it's an artificial island. It was built years ago to store fresh water. It was never used. They must hiv meant to build more 'cause that one's known as number four.' Lara rested her hands on her unborn.

'Amazing,' said Campbell.

Renie Blacking hadn't been able or willing to tell him anything. Campbell wasn't surprised. She was caught between her husband, her daughter and her job. He'd taken the long route round by the road to the Blacking's cottage and he felt stiff. He rotated his shoulders. He had one more call to make before he took himself back to the office. He hoped the laboratory would still be open. After all, Geraldine Franson might not have made it to her holiday and such a lead had to be checked out as soon as possible.

As he drove he heard over the radio that DS Bridget Jenner was back from her course. He was keen to tell her Lara Elves's story. But somehow he couldn't shake off the idea that his trip to the monastery had been as curious as trying to make a journey with an old map on which none of the new roads were marked.

Chapter 4

The light from the stars and moon picked out the white block of the laboratory down on the edge of the river for Campbell as he came out of the woods. His headlights followed the weave of the road to the car park where a bright security beam flicked on and made him squint.

Still with unfocussed eyes, he plied his usual pleasantries in the office at the girl behind the strengthened glass screen. Along with his, 'It's dark early now,' he took in her appearance. Today, he decided, must be a small, dark haired woman sort of day, as this was the third one he'd come across – if he included the deceased. He shook off such thoughts as light headedness caused by his cold and adjusted the paper poppy on his jacket.

Having scrutinized his identity card, the girl, who called herself Carroll Enderby, pressed a button below Campbell's eye-level and let him into a small interview room.

He settled his rear into the low soft seat. Carroll Enderby took the one opposite and leaned forward resting her forearms on her knees and clutching her hands together. Campbell wondered if her tension was normal, "I'm talking to the police," tension or something more.

As he looked at her he realised that not only was it a small, dark haired woman sort of day but that fact accentuated the uselessness of his information. The only description he could give of the dead woman found on Catstail Sandbank would not only describe Carroll Enderby, in front of him, but Lara Elves and, indeed, many other women. But it was all he had so he tried it out on her.

Her face paled showing up the fine freckles over her sharp cheek-bones and small pointed nose. He didn't think the picture on her identification badge did her justice.

'Geraldine,' she said as if the word had got caught up in her throat.

'Geraldine who?' asked Campbell guessing the answer to be Franson. But he was surprised at how quickly she'd picked up on the possibility of her colleague being dead.

'Geraldine Franson, Inspector, could be my sister. But it can't be her, she's gone on holiday. She's been away a week and she's got another two weeks left. She's going to Spain and Africa.' Carroll started to bite her nails and jiggle her knees. Her deep tones gave her words a strength which Campbell found appealing.

'I'm sorry this is upsetting, but it is only one line of enquiry.' Campbell used his lyrical Scottish accent to try and sooth her. 'I just want to check that she got off on her holiday all right.' He waited for this to sink in and then asked to see Geraldine's boss.

'Stranfield?' she asked.

'Aye.'

Still trembling she went to fetch him.

Stranfield entered, like a cockerel defending his territory, thought Campbell. His receding red hair was preened into a crest while a red beard guarded his chin. Campbell told himself off again for being flippant.

He felt himself stretching his body to its limits to try and meet Stranfield's size, and he held his hand with equal firmness when they shook hands. He matched the bold square look Stranfield gave him. The high temples above cool green eyes challenged Campbell's intelligence and the large powerful nose gave the impression Stranfield had just won some unspoken argument.

Carroll Enderby followed him in, her head cast down.

'May I take your full name?' asked Campbell seeing that Stranfield chose to remain standing while he sat to ease his note making.

'Bertram Stranfield – no middle name. I'm very busy, Inspector.'

'He thinks Geraldine might be dead,' said Carroll Enderby biting her lip. Campbell noted the crack in her voice.

'I haven't said that,' said Campbell.

'I know,' said Carroll.

'Go and get a cup of tea, Carroll,' said Stranfield. He had a hard edge to his voice. 'And make one for us at the same time.'

When Carroll had gone Campbell said, 'Perhaps I might borrow a photograph of Geraldine Franson.' He looked at Stranfield's badge. Even the dulling effect of a photo-booth had not taken out the angry glare from his eyes. 'Her address and any details of her friends and family would help,' he added.

'We don't bring our domestic lives into work here,' said Stranfield. 'I'm short staffed with Geraldine away, Inspector. We've managed one week without her and I have to cope for another two. I'm sure you understand.' He turned to the door. 'Carroll will give you any details we have on file.'

Stranfield pulled the door open sharply making Carroll Enderby, laden with tea cups on the other side, stumble into the room. Campbell thought she ought to have fallen but she regained her balance with a gymnastic twist of the body. Even so tea sloshed over the saucers. Stranfield swore and left.

'I'm afraid he's short of manners at the best of times,' said Carroll.

Campbell wondered if that was why her nerves were shot.

'Does Geraldine Franson have any relatives or friends?' he asked.

'She's never said. She only ever talks about her work. I can give you what we've got.'

Leaving the un-mopped tea to cool on the coffee table Campbell allowed Carroll Enderby to take him back into the reception lobby.

In the moment she was gone to fetch the information she had about Geraldine, Campbell felt heat well up in his chest. When she passed him the piece of paper she'd written the address on, he shivered.

'It's going to be a cold night,' she said.

He heard her. But he felt as if he wasn't alive. His illness seemed to be robbing him of reality. Her voice sounded like a distant tin drum. Some remote part of him said, 'Goodbye,' and he made his way to the car. Every part of his body seemed to be screaming at him to stop, while some deep rooted Scottish soul pushed him on to get back to the office to pass this information on to DS Bridget Jenner.

Campbell stretched his arms above his head. He felt better now he was in his office. Ordinarily he hated his office, so he knew he wasn't well. DC Sally Garden was elsewhere checking the records on Brother Michael and Brother Joshua. The thought of the big monk made him feel small and sick again. And, his lack of health brought him back to Dr Hok.

He had said it would probably be up to Campbell to find out how the woman on the sandbank had died and at that moment the only way to decide that seemed to be to find out who she was – this body with no face and just one finger, no jewellery, no cards, no tattoos.

He'd sent DC Flagg to the autopsy. Campbell couldn't manage the smells of the chemical preservatives mixed with disinfectants along with the odour of rotting meat. And, he found it hard to like Flagg. On his way through the outer office he'd noticed how the young officer had occupied more space than was strictly his. Office furniture had been moved creating his own sectioned off corner. When he'd asked Jenner about it she'd said she hadn't time to worry about it. Her steady blue eyes had remained concentrated at her desk until she'd compiled lists, time tables, tide tables and maps.

But right now Campbell had an almost uncontrollable urge to shove it all in the bin – especially the unpleasant photographs of the lacerated face and body. He brought his hands down onto the table and shuffled the pictures. He may have been a policeman for twenty five years but he was still a human being. They revolted him. Dr Hok thought it likely that the cuts had been done after death which helped him cope.

'She hasn't been reported as a missing person locally,' said Jenner, taking one of the pictures from the table and pinning it with the same measured control she applied to everything. Campbell thought she could have been doing the washing up for all the effect their content had on her.

'Check nationally,' suggested Campbell knowing she was already planning to do so. 'She wouldn't be the first visitor to walk out on the sandbanks and get caught by the tide.' He blew his nose. 'What do you think of Lara Elves's story?'

'I've got a list of fishermen and dock workers to get through. It'll be easier in the morning to check them out and find fishermen. They'll be either coming in or getting ready to go out on the tide.' Jenner tapped her book of tide tables. ' Even if they don't confirm Lara Elves's story, they may have seen something.'

'Are there any houses over-looking the river?' asked Campbell.

'The banks are built up too high all the way along there for anyone except a walker to have noticed anything,' replied Jenner. 'And if the people Lara Elves saw were dumping a body under the bridge then cars going over the top wouldn't have seen much either.'

'Someone might have seen something. Arrange for some notices to go up for witnesses and a press release asking for anyone who's seen anything unusual in the last two weeks.'

'Yes, Sir.'

'And what do you think of Lara's story?' Campbell fumbled inside his trouser pocket for his handkerchief.

'I find the connection between her working at the monastery and her husband and father working on the sandbank a bit of a strange coincidence under the circumstances. I would like to talk to her myself tomorrow, if that's all right?'

'Of course,' he said. 'But this is a small, long established community. You can find members of any one local family almost everywhere in and around Saint John's Town. You've told me that yourself on more than one occasion.'

Not only had Jenner organised all the paperwork, Campbell realised, but she'd read Garden's report – and probably all the others – too. Such efficiency he found, because of his cold, slightly intimidating. Suddenly he regretted his lost lunch at home. And that brought him back to Jack Wren. The need to write up the attempted suicide had been forgotten in the rush to start investigating the body on the sandbank.

Having filled in the box for the address on his computer screen at which the event took place, Campbell fiddled with the keyboard. 'I think I'll go and see Jack Wren,' he said remembering the plastic bag with the empty padded box and tweezers in the car.

Jenner's tightly bound blond hair moved as she looked up. 'I'm sorry. I forgot to tell you. There was a message left for you while you were out. He's been flown to a diving hospital for treatment – pressurised oxygen, or so they say. He's still unconscious.'

'Oh,' said Campbell reaching for his great coat. 'Was any jewellery found in Mrs Agatha Spier's garage, Jenner?'

'No, Sir,' she said.

She frowned at him but his arms and legs ached and his head was throbbing so he didn't explain. He put the pain down to his walk across the sandbank and his cold. The plastic bag would have to wait for now.

'Do you suspect that it might not be attempted suicide?' asked Jenner.

'No. The garage was locked from the inside.' He opened the office door. 'Goodnight, Jenner.' He didn't wait for her reply. His mind could not think any more unless it slept.

Carroll Enderby put on her white mesh bonnet over her short dark hair and her boiler-suit over her small supple limbs, then her mask, over-shoes and nitrile gloves. She mustn't leave any dust in the laboratory and she liked the impersonality of this clothing. She'd even unpicked her name tape from the front. Not that anyone was going to see her tonight and if they did the clothes made a reasonable disguise.

She was beginning not to like people. The policeman with the pale eyes this morning had frightened her. And then there was that Scottish Inspector here this afternoon wanting to know about Geraldine. Could Geraldine be the dead body on Catstail Sandbank? Surely the police couldn't suspect her of anything? It couldn't be Geraldine anyway. Geraldine was on holiday.

Carroll had wanted to tell Campbell about the pale green-eyed policeman but she'd been too scared of her own wrong doings. She still couldn't shake off the thought that he'd followed her because of them. And she'd wondered when the Scottish Inspector had helped her with the spilt tea, as she wondered now, whether he also knew about her.

This would be the last time she gave Derek Browme any information. She couldn't risk being caught. He hadn't come up with the money he'd promised. He said he'd be able to get it from a national newspaper. But she hadn't found anything about the micro-chip they were working on that was damaging to the environment or anything about the running of this company that was in any way underhand. It had been set up by Stranfield to develop the special micro-chip. She'd been silly to give Derek Browme that list of investors and now she wished that at least she'd looked at them. She was risking her job for nothing.

Getting in tonight had been tricky. She'd parked in the woods and waited for the security firm that checked the lab a couple of times during the night to come back past her from their first visit, before pulling out of the woods and down the narrow open road leading to the laboratory. She hadn't any other way of getting in without firing up the perimeter security lights. She'd have to risk going up to the front door under the fixed lighting.

But how she wanted extra money – more than her job gave her. And to get that she needed information. She'd run through Geraldine's and Stranfield's desk drawers, trawled all the files in the computer and there was only one other place to try: the secure filing in the room on the other side of the laboratory. Stranfield had decided to have it there, away from easy access, but it meant every visit involved dressing up and wrapping each folder in a plastic bag to bring it out. Certain information, he'd said at her induction, was too important to keep on computers. It seemed to her by that he meant everything.

The white surfaces of the laboratory reflected the cold moon as Carroll walked past the sealed glass window looking across the river to the Wash. She didn't need her torch. She put Geraldine's key and the security code into the lock. Geraldine was so trusting. She left all her keys in the top drawer of her desk unlocked, and Carroll had access to the code because Geraldine always sent her to get the files. Putting the light on she settled down to look through all the paperwork about the micro-chip. She felt safer in here. There were no windows so she couldn't be seen from outside.

Her cold fingers fumbled over the stiff beige card. She pulled out photographs of electron microscopic images of the chip. It was a truly beautiful piece of engineering. "Even I can see that," thought Carroll. And then she noticed the dating on the pages. These were old pictures. She hadn't put them away. They were in the wrong order – the latest dated item should have been on top when the file was opened, but these were reversed. Stranfield didn't allow the files to be tampered with. And Carroll knew she hadn't had them out. That only left Geraldine.

Carroll's mind raced. Why would she do that? She turned the pages over looking for a clue. They were in firmly, so they hadn't fallen out and been put back in the wrong order. Someone would have complained to her about that. Why would Geraldine take them out? To look at the papers more carefully? Perhaps. But there were no newer pictures of the chip printed and though she wasn't a scientist she knew it had been developed further, so why would Geraldine have done this? And, she knew how Stranfield was obsessive about stray file contents, so he certainly had not left this mess. Then a number written on the back of one of the prints caught her attention. She recognised the file reference straight away – the suppliers' folder.

As Carroll pulled it out of the drawer the bulging papers slid from their fastener and fell to her feet. Scrabbling delivery notes from companies for such items as test-tubes and nitrogen up into an untidy pile she saw on top a torn piece of paper with a scribbled note on it. The green ink only used by Stranfield, who never ordered anything himself, made her pick it up and read it.

'Leave it alone, Geraldine,' was all that was left of what was clearly a longer message.

'Leave what alone?' asked Carroll aloud. Again she turned the paper over as she'd done the microchip prints, and she saw a phone number written in black biro in Geraldine's hand. This time she decided it must be a phone number from the pattern and quantity of digits. She didn't recognise it instantly although it was local.

Sitting back on her heels Carroll tried to recall Geraldine's behaviour before she went on holiday. Her senior scientist had been remote. She remembered her grey eyes reflecting the images of the Wash as she'd stared out of the window. She knew how much Geraldine loved her work to the point where her dedication annoyed her. If only Geraldine would press for higher wages she would have more success in trying to up hers. And then she wouldn't have to do this.

Then she recalled the angry voices of Geraldine and Stranfield arguing one lunch time when Carroll had come back early. She'd never heard Geraldine in such a rage. And Stranfield liked to tie people up with obligation, commitment – entwining Geraldine and herself in threads of sometimes quiet and sometimes less quiet bullying. And now he was yelling at Geraldine. If they'd been arguing over the chip, she wondered, would Geraldine unwrap herself from Stranfield's words and look elsewhere to sell her brain power? Would she be capable of selling all she knew about the chip to someone else? Yes, that had to be it. That would fit the dishevelled folder, Geraldine's moods, her extended holiday.

Anyway – she pulled herself upright – this number might be Geraldine's contact. Carroll realised that she no longer needed Derek Browme and his newspapers. He could take his thinning hair and gold rimmed glasses and jump in the river for all she cared. She must have access to all the same material Geraldine could get and she could collect it anytime she wanted. All she had to do was keep looking. Glancing at the clock on the wall she realised it was time to go. She put the file straight and put it back. The secure filing room had to look untouched. She slid the note and number inside her polythene glove. She would try phoning it tomorrow.

The risk of getting caught was getting greater with every second. Safety meant being beyond the road leading to the laboratory before the security firm made their second check of the premises.

In her mind she converted the telephone number into money – and smiled.

The red digital numbers of his bed-side clock said 03.30. If he'd said goodnight to his teenagers or kissed his wife, Margaret, he couldn't remember. His head was completely fuddled. He started to cough. His chest gripped him. He thought his ribs had turned into claws and he wondered why he deserved such punishment.

He became aware of Margaret's angular bones as she rolled out of bed and put the main light on. His eyes hurt. The coughing subsided. He looked into her face as she examined his. Another fit of coughing caught him and he rolled his head between his knees. He could hardly breathe. He wanted to tell Margaret he was all right, but couldn't.

By the time the doctor arrived the wave of stifled breathing had eased to be replaced by a coughing fit. So, Campbell found himself wheezing that he would live, just as the doctor applied his stethoscope to the Scotsman's chest.

'Your wife tells me you filled your lungs with toxic fumes today, Raymond?'

'Car exhaust fumes,' Campbell managed to reply.

'And you had a cold brewing by the look of it?'

'Stiff from walking on a sandbank.' Campbell coughed again.

'Given yourself a touch of pneumonia,' said the doctor. 'Antibiotics should sort you out. I'll be back to check on you tomorrow. Until then you do not move from this bed.'

Campbell rolled over and pulled the quilt around his ears.

'Did you hear me, Campbell?'

'He heard you, Doctor,' said Margaret.

A distant voice in Campbell's head wondered whether it was the antibiotics, his temperature or the strange happenings of the day that caused him to watch a dream sweep towards him as his wife and doctor left the room.

He dreamt of Brother Michael and Brother Joshua rolling like lovers on the sea bank; of Polly Browme standing next to a fuming garage cradling a baby in her arms. She was dangling a pair of tweezers over the swaddled babe. The metal caught the light and angled it down to the baby's face and when he looked closely a tiny Lara Elves smiled out from the wrappings. And he dreamt of digging a hole in the garden for his pond. But there was so much earth, surely more than could have come from such a small hole. Finally, he saw Jack Wren recovered from the exhaust fumes in the garage. He was standing over the body in the Wash where Curran Elves had stood. He wished himself away from the dream. He wished himself better, and he wished to know who the dead woman was.

Chapter 5

Curran Elves ordered himself another pint and watched the breasts of the bar maid held inside a low-cut, body hugging top. They reminded him of the mounds of sand he'd seen stacked along the new road being built beyond the suspension bridge. The smell of urine and bleach caught in his nose as he spread a handful of change on the gnarled oak surface, leant on the bar and curled one bandy leg behind the other. The beer was good after his day on the Wash.

'How much, Pet?' he asked her. She looked soft to hold, warm to bed, not like Lara. 'Can I take you out? When are you free?' He knew he was pushing his luck.

He noted Pet's breasts blush when she pulled the money she needed from the heap.

'What's this?' she asked.

Curran looked down at the scattered pile from his pocket. In the centre a dark green gem reflected the shaded lights of the saloon bar.

'How did that get there?' he asked.

'It's beautiful,' said Pet. 'You've had too much, if you can't remember how you got that.'

'It belonged to my grandmother,' he said scooping his change and the sparkling stone back into his pocket. 'Did you say you'd be free on Monday?'

'No I didn't,' said Pet arching an eyebrow. Curran Elves was pleased to hear the bar door click open and wheeze shut. Pet just might leave off about the jewel if she had another customer. He followed her gaze. A vast red-bearded man in a suit was strutting towards them from the self-closing door.

Curran always felt his eyesight improved and his memory was more alert with a few beers. So he wasn't at all surprised that he recognised the boss of that filthy laboratory as soon as he introduced himself. The tort tones of an

41

educated man from the South East of England angered Curran.

'You're ruining me,' he told Stranfield. 'All that filthy stuff you put in the Wash is killing the shell fish. I know your sort: friends who are members of parliament, ministers. You lot think you can do what you like.'

'Can I buy you a drink, Curran Elves?' asked Stranfield.

'No.'

'I'll have a whisky and my friend will have the same,' said Stranfield.

'He don't sound like no friend of yours,' said Pet.

'It's all right, Pet,' said Curran. 'I'll give the man a hearing and then I'll punch his lights out.'

'Not in here you won't,' said Pet.

Curran watched her take Stranfield's money.

'I hear you found a body on Catstail Sand Bank,' said Stranfield.

'Where did you hear that from?' asked Curran.

'Everyone knows.' Stranfield spread his large hands on the bar. 'This isn't such a big town,' he said.

'That was you, was it?' Pet asked Curran as she stretched to get glasses for the whisky.

'Let's sit in comfort over here,' said Stranfield waving at the pub's holed but clean red cloth seats as if the room belonged to him. He clearly didn't want others to hear their conversation.

Curran felt he'd been standing propped against the bar long enough so he waved to Pet and followed the whiskies being carried by the red head and whiskers.

'Tell me about it,' said Stranfield. 'What was the dead woman like?'

'You're sick.' Curran took his seat opposite Stranfield. 'No-one in their right mind would want to know that.'

'Let me put it another way: what did you see?'

'I told the police what I saw. I showed it to them. It was a nightmare. And I'm not going to talk about it. Not for a whisky, anyway.'

Stranfield reached into the inside of his jacket.

'Money won't make me tell either,' said Curran through his teeth. He wasn't going to show this lump of rotting fish how much he would like to add a roll of paper notes to his pocket. 'The police won't let me talk about it.'

'The police think it might have been one of the women who work for me. They could soon find out what you feel about my laboratory, Elves. Is that a better lubrication than whisky?'

'Tell them what you like.' Curran felt sick with keeping back the force he wanted to give the words. 'You'll tell them anyway. I may be poor but I hint stupid. I think you know where you can put your threats.'

'Hush, man. You'll get us thrown out. I need to know. If nothing else, can you tell me if you found anything out there – anything unusual?'

'I think a dead body without any face is unusual enough,' said Curran thrusting his arm over the table knocking the glasses across the room. He felt the follow through roll him off his seat and onto the floor. He knew he shouldn't have said that. Hell.

Strong nails dug through his jersey from the hands that hauled him to his feet. He looked towards the face of the hands' owner. Pet scowled back at him.

'Enough,' she said. 'I want you both out of here now.'

The glare from the late dawn of an early Saturday morning in November caught across DC Flagg's pale green eyes. He protected them with the sunglasses from his top pocket. He didn't want to wait for Jenner, but she was bringing the locksmith. He looked up at the block of flats converted from an old brick warehouse.

Fancy old Campbell being sick. That was typical of him. Winging Scots Git. Leave all the dross jobs for the likes of him and Jenner. Shitty women sergeants. He could only pretend to obey her, only appear polite.

He spotted her coming from her car with that Garden creature. Jenner always looked so tight with her neat yellow hair, he thought. And why do women always have to have some other woman to go about with? You'd think those two were joined at the hip. And where's this locksmith then?

'There's a caretaker,' said Jenner as soon as she reached him. 'We don't need a locksmith.'

Stop smiling, woman, thought Flagg.

'Geraldine's flat is on the top floor,' said Jenner, 'but there's a lift. With Campbell off sick I've got some others to go down to the harbour and get their stories. If anything crops up to confirm, or otherwise, Lara's story they're going to flag it up. Ah, here comes the caretaker now. I did phone him to say we'd be here at this time. Excellent.'

'Come on. Let's be getting on with it,' Flagg muttered, so low no-one could have heard him. He gripped the handle to the main door of the flats and shoved his weight against the door. It barely rattled.

'What did the Coroner have to say about our body on Catstail Sand

Bank?' asked Jenner.

'The report's on Campbell's desk,' said Flagg.

'But you went to the autopsy?' queried Garden.

'I did.' Flagg watched Garden flush with temper down to the roots of her frizzy brown hair. Got you, Bitch, he thought. He wasn't going to tell them a thing.

'Mr Stock,' said Jenner nodding at a small man in his sixties wearing a flat peaked hat and a dark uniform as he trotted across the car park towards them.

'Can you get us into flat 6?' Flagg asked Mr Stock controlling his voice. He was pleased at how normal and efficient he could sound when he tried.

'I hope Miss Franson is alright,' said Mr Stock.

'We all do,' said Jenner.

Mr Stock unlocked the main door and suggested they went up ahead of him as he had to collect the key from his room in the basement.

In the lift Flagg spread his legs and pulled his shoulders back. 'Campbell's a prat,' he said.

'Why?' asked Jenner.

'I called on Lara Elves' mother, Renie Blacking, yesterday because he told me to.'

'I see,' said Jenner.

'You know?' asked Flagg.

Jenner nodded.

'Campbell had already been,' said Flagg. 'She gave me a real mouth full.'

'He wasn't well,' said Garden.

'I don't see what that has got to do with it. He made me look a fool.'

Jenner smiled and Flagg wanted to smash her face in. Instead he thumped the inside of the lift.

Once Mr Stock had let them into the flat he was dismissed and Flagg shouldered past Jenner and Garden pulling on a pair of polythene gloves. The living room smelt of paint, varnish, new carpet and polish.

'Expensive,' said Jenner.

Flagg watched her look around the room. 'I'll do the bedroom,' said Flagg.

'No, I'll go in there. You can do in here. If she's only on holiday she will want a flat to come back to. Remember that.'

Flagg felt himself flinch: "Cow. But then," he thought, "she can have the flimsy underwear and the books by the bed." He smiled because he would get the desk.

'DC Garden can do the bathroom and kitchen,' said Jenner.

'Right,' said Flagg turning to the modern desk complete with computer and unlocked - he quickly discovered – desk drawers. Papers, obviously household bills, filled a couple of folders in the bottom drawer, the top drawer held stationary but the middle drawer contained an address book and diary. He had barely turned the hard cover of the diary when Jenner called from the bedroom.

'I've found a letter from her mother. I can't believe the address.' She came into the living room. 'Is there an address book in there I can check it against. The name's Agatha Spier.'

A yellow paper was thrust in front of Flagg. One of those printed address labels with a picture of a cottage was stuck on to the top left hand corner.

'What's so special about that?'

'It's where Inspector Campbell saved that old man in the garage.'

'He might not have saved him yet,' reminded Flagg. 'Jack Wren is still out cold.'

'Look, it's signed, Mum,' persisted Jenner.

She turned the paper over and pointed to the scrawled ink line along the bottom.

'I wonder why she should write when she lives so near,' said Garden joining them from the kitchen. 'What does it say?'

Jenner read:

*Dear Gerry, I couldn't catch you on the phone last night and your answer machine seems to be on the blink. I did want to say to you to have a really good trip to Spain before I go away myself so I'm just dropping you this note. Love Mum.*

'What's the date on it?' asked Garden.

'The day before Geraldine Franson went on holiday,' said Jenner.

'And her mother couldn't contact her?' said Garden.

'It certainly seems that way,' said Jenner.

'Agatha Spier must've remarried to have a different name to her single daughter,' observed Garden.

'Did you open the letter?' asked Flagg taking it from Jenner. He'd had enough of these clacking women. What did Franson's mother matter? She'd hardly be the one to dump her own daughter in the drink.

'The letter was open and slotted inside her bedside book,' said Jenner taking it back. 'So presumably she'd received and read it. But there's nothing we can really do with that information at the moment. But we could listen to the answer machine.'

Flagg looked at the phone in its cradle. The message box had a red zero shining out at him. 'There are no messages listed,' he said and pressed the button to hear if there was anything recorded. It clicked for a few moments but no voices came out. 'Her mother was right.'

'What we could do with,' said Jenner, 'is the name of her holiday company so we can check that she actually got off to Spain OK.'

Flagg slung her the address book. 'You look, then,' he said as he turned back to the diary. The pages confirmed Geraldine's holiday dates as the first three weeks in November. He called out the information to Jenner who'd returned to the bedroom having placed Mrs Spier's letter in a plastic bag.

'We'll have to take the diary with us,' called Jenner. 'Pop it in one of those bags for now and write it on the receipt.'

Flagg peeled apart the sides of the polythene bag and was about to slot the book between them when an envelope slid out of the bottom of the diary. Without looking at it Flagg pulled it out and slipped it in his pocket. He'd wanted to get back at Campbell for making him look a fool over Mrs Blacking and now he had something that might just give him an edge over that blasted Scottish Inspector. And, more than that, he felt good about having something no-one else knew about.

Sitting back in Geraldine's swivel chair his gaze travelled up and across a cabinet covered in photographs. There were men and women and children, the usual mixed bunch of families. He picked out a likely Agatha Spier for Jenner, fat, blue-rinsed hair, like his own mother. Then his attention was taken by a picture of Geraldine Franson. (He recognised her from that terrible photo Campbell had brought back from her office.) She was standing next to a withered, bald chap – he could have been her grandfather. And they were both wearing remembrance poppies on their coats.

He thought of the pile of blood red artificial poppies sitting on the front reception desk at the police station, and the argument he'd had because Sergeant Porter'd said he ought to buy one for Remembrance Day. Why should he? He didn't give a toss.

He wondered when the photograph of Geraldine and the pale man had been taken. Coats took longer to date than dresses but her hair was long and wavy, not like the work's photo where it was reduced to a bob.

With his envelope from Geraldine's diary in his pocket he felt almost generous about telling Jenner about the photograph. It was, after all, a fairly useless and obvious piece of information. But when she returned announcing the name of the travel agent Geraldine had booked with before he could speak, he said nothing.

He was even pleased when Garden found Geraldine's car keys in a kitchen drawer. It meant he could leave the flat with his envelope secreted from them. Gathering the bagged books, pictures and papers together he saw Jenner pick up the receipt.

'I'll put the diary on too,' she said.

'Oh yeah,' said Flagg. He watched her sign the receipt and leave it on the table in the middle of the room.

'Geraldine has a company car,' said Jenner. 'It was one of the details Campbell was able to get from her work.'

'Good old Campbell,' said Flagg. He enjoyed the cool hate with which his sarcasm was received by the women.

'Not only,' continued Jenner, 'will we be able to spot her car but now we'll get inside it. That also means she either hired a car or was driven to the airport, giving us other leads to check.'

Flagg spotted the car in a parking space reserved for the flats. Jenner took the area by the driver's seat to search while he checked the passenger's side; Garden looked in the boot and underneath the car. There was nothing. It was clean and the only sign of use was some music. Squatting, he leaned back to watch Jenner stand up.

'DC Flagg, you can take the papers back to the office and contact Geraldine's travel agent. We need all the information we can get. DC Garden you can start working your way through her phone book to see if anyone in it knows where she is. I'm going to see Lara Elves about her story. After all, Geraldine may not be the body on Catstail Sand Bank, and Campbell will want to know who it is when he gets back.'

During the journey to the police station Flagg failed to speak to Garden and he was pleased that she made no attempt to speak to him. He smiled. A strange strength filled his limbs and his head as he thought about what might be in the envelope in his pocket.

He wondered what she would think if she knew about his little hobby of using a car he'd kitted out in police trim and of him donning his old uniform devoid of numbers and of the way he meted out a little extra policing to the public in his own time.

*   *   *

Comfortable with her lunched stomach and her morning's work, Jenner pulled into the grounds of the once substantial family house, which was now an old people's home, or residential home for the elderly – as she'd been corrected by the matron, sorry, manager, on the phone. A few telephone enquiries had found Lara not to be at work at the monastery or at her home in a scruffy part of St James Town but here, visiting her husband's paternal grandmother, Charlotte Elves, as she always did on a Saturday.

As Jenner'd sipped her last drop of coffee from her flask cup the information gathered from the docks had come through to her on the radio. Now what had been a routine call had become essential to furthering the enquiry.

DS Jenner straightened her jacket as she walked from the car to the door and read the sign posted by the bell. No, she didn't have a cold, so she didn't have to call another day as outlined in the notice and, anyway, she wasn't really visiting any of the old people.

A woman carer came and had her sign in a visitors' book as she took in the vaulted ceilings, heavy wooden doors and level block flooring. Beyond one such door, which stood open, she saw the afternoon sun pouring through vast conservatory windows. The light picked out old ladies sitting staring at their knees, fumbling with newspapers, sleeping or talking to their visitors among the pot plants. As she got closer she could see that they each wore a dark red poppy on their cardigan as she did on the lapel of her jacket.

She was struck by the history of the people in front of her. Perhaps they remembered little of the Second World War now, but she thought she could see it carved into the lines of their faces. 'They like it in here, in the sun,' said the carer. 'Now there's Charlotte, and Lara's there too.'

'Thank you,' said Jenner hoping the carer would go away.

But instead the woman stepped up to Lara Elves and said, 'Have you tried it yet.'

Lara shook her head. 'No I hint,' she said.

'We really have had some very good results with some of the residents. It's the familiarity of the object which fires their memories.'

'I don't know,' said Lara. 'I like her the way she is. She used to live in a cottage with cold floors and wet coming through the walls before she came here. She used to boil onions for her dinner. What has she got to remember?'

Jenner felt torn between the urgency of her interview with Lara and the gentle softness on old Charlotte's face.

'It would really give her such joy to remember something from her past. I've seen it so many times,' said the carer. 'What have you brought?'

'This,' said Lara Elves pulling from her cloth bag a small pewter box. The mouldings appeared to Jenner to be of fish and boats.

The carer nodded encouragingly. 'It's beautiful. Give it to her then.'

Lara Elves pulled Charlotte's skirt down to cover her cream coloured slip and placed the box on the crimplene lap. Charlotte's crooked fingers left the edge of her chair and fumbled towards the box still held steady by Lara's hand. She took it from her grand-daughter-in-law and held it up to her milky eyes.

'Why, it's so pretty,' said the old woman. Jenner thought her frail voice was like a sigh from another world. Then she saw Charlotte's face change. A shadow of knowledge cast a frown across her forehead and puckered her toothless gums.

'What is it, Gran?' asked Lara Elves.

'I know this thing,' said Charlotte.

'What is it?' asked Lara.

Charlotte Elves fiddled with the catch until one of her yellowed thumb nails was able to prize open the lid. Once inside, Jenner felt herself peeping with the others into its red velvet lining. There was nothing in it. Charlotte's face crumpled. A misery seemed to cave it in, taking all the life and energy that had been there a moment ago away. Jenner wanted to fold an arm about the old woman as tears started to dribble incontinently down her face but Lara was already there sobbing with her grandmother-in-law.

Suddenly Jenner had no more time for this. There was an unidentified woman lying dead in a mortuary fridge. She had to talk to Lara Elves.

'Lara Elves,' she said touching her shoulder.

'What do you want?' Lara swung her head round, still touching Charlotte's knee with her right hand.

'I need to speak with you about the story you gave Inspector Campbell.'

'Why?'

'Perhaps outside?' Jenner watched the carer move to comfort Charlotte. The formal garden still supported a few chrysanthemums and wilting asters, but they were to be seen by most of the residents from behind glass. Jenner thought that a shame. She turned to Lara.

'I hint seen her cry since we took her from her old cottage,' said Lara

Elves. 'She wouldn't leave because she'd lived there with her husband before the sea took him. And she'd lived there with her son, but the sea took him too. And the sea took her son's wife. That only left her grandson, my Curran. And she brought him up on her own in that house. Do you know she kept everything ready for them if they came home? Pyjamas still lay ready for her men folk to put on and a nightie for her son's wife. I think all that death sent her dolally. It wasn't as if they hadn't found the bodies. '

'Can you tell me again what happened when you saw that thing which looked like a body being put in the river? Where was it?'

'Under the bridge. I told Inspector Campbell all this.'

'He's not well.'

'My dad told me to show her that trinket box. He said that was hers. I bet he knew that would upset her. I'll get him.'

'It seems strange to me that your husband and your father both work out on the sand banks,' said Jenner.

'Not really. I used to walk out there when I was a little girl with my dad. That's how I met Curran. Anyway I don't see that it's none of your business. I'll get my dad for upsetting Gran. She's all the family Curran's got.'

'Lara, we can't find anybody to confirm your story down at the docks.'

'Well, you wouldn't would you. They'd all've been out on their boats. It was nearly low tide. All the fishermen and the cargo ships go up and down the river at high tide.'

Jenner wanted to hide her embarrassment at her oversight so looked away. She knew Campbell would have been totally unabashed.


Carroll Enderby unhooked the kneeler from the pew in front of her. There was barely room between the pews for her to kneel on its embroidered cross and maroon back-ground. She could not talk to God sitting on a seat. Who was she trying to fool? Not the frail women filling the rows in front of her, nor the men standing stiff and straight holding wreaths of poppies. She couldn't even trick herself. She knew her visit to church had nothing to do with God. She couldn't remember when she'd last been to church on a Sunday. But she'd made the time to come before getting ready for her course at Newington University the next day.

Her small frame made it easy to lean on the wood in front of her and bury her face in her hands. Sweat prickled her skin and she shivered. She recognised her symptoms as fear not flu. She should never have phoned that number she'd found in the office file. That simple act had brought her into dealings far more dangerous than any she'd had with that journalist, Browme.

What had that dark voice on the other end of the line said to her? It sounded like something from the Bible... 'The axe is already at the root of the trees, and every tree that does not produce good fruit will be cut down and thrown into the fire.' She'd so readily said that she would undercut Geraldine's price, that she could get anything Geraldine could get. The voice had told her to go to this church at this time to be told more.

And she'd said to him to look out for a small, thin dark-haired woman in a yellow coat without a poppy.

No wonder Geraldine didn't try for more money with Stranfield, thought Carroll. She had plenty of money coming in from this weirdo. Carroll uncovered her eyes. The church was filling up with the congregation for the Remembrance service. She thought that the dark colour of the paper poppies was so unlike the vermillion of the poppies that lined the fields in summer. These were more like dead poppies hanging from the lapels of the congregation.

The service started and Carroll was slightly surprised at herself for coming here. Yet she had to put the strange biblical quotation to the back of her mind. Without money she was nothing. This man would surely make a deal with her which would, at last, make her rich. But all the same, she felt perhaps it might've been safer to pretend to be Geraldine on the phone. But she was on holiday, or was she?

Two thoughts struck Carroll as she looked at the rows of dark coats and suits. The man on the phone could think she'd killed Geraldine or, indeed, he could be Geraldine's murderer.

No, Geraldine couldn't be dead, she told herself. She loved her, really she did. Someone you loved couldn't just die. They mustn't. She loved Geraldine's anger and disloyalty to Stranfield before she went on holiday. Carroll felt sure now she'd made a mistake. She should never have made that phone call. She shouldn't have come here. She had to leave. But people had started to file out up the aisle to the War Memorial outside.

A wheel-chair bound monk filled the narrow gap at the end of her pew. He was followed by a vast monk whose robe was too short and left his ankles bare. Carroll looked for a gap. More bodies crushed forward. Then she saw Stranfield's red hair. What was he doing here? She looked down quickly hoping he hadn't spotted her. She watched his gleaming brogues walk by. She looked up again ready to smile her way into the line of people.

Her face froze. Two people down she could see the spiky blond head and the pale eyes of the policeman who'd pursued her on her way to work the other morning. Even though he was wearing a suit instead of a uniform she was sure it was him. Suddenly her hand fell from the top of the pew in front of her which she'd been using to steady herself. She half sat, half fell back onto the bench seat catching a pile of hymn books stacked there. They tumbled across the aisle. Two women, one neat and blond and about Geraldine's age and another with frizzy brown hair picked them up and helped her stand. Yes, she was fine, she said to them.

Carroll looked around. The policeman had gone. He'd passed around her accident, she presumed, and left the church with the rest of the congregation. Then the frizzy haired woman passed her a piece of paper she'd picked up from the floor and asked Carroll if it was hers.

'Yes, thank you,' she said. She hadn't seen it before in her life. But she guessed it must've come from the man she'd spoken to on the phone. The thought of the money she could get for the chip seemed to devour her fear.

'I'll be fine,' she reassured the women, her voice breaking. She sat down. Left on her own in the church she read the note.

Chapter 6

'Send my apologies to Flagg,' said Campbell to Jenner. He watched her standing beside the bed as stiff and neat as if she were on parade.

At last Margaret had been unable to keep her business at bay and had left his sick bed to visit her accountant. His son and daughter were at school. Thus he'd slipped Jenner into the house despite his wife's orders of no work. Jenner'd been instructed on the need for complete secrecy.

'Flagg's a strange bloke,' said Jenner. 'He was all against the Remembrance Day stuff and then when he heard someone was needed to represent the station he put himself forward.'

'Did you go?'

'Yes, so did Garden. There was an enormous crowd. Garden pointed out to me Curran Elves and Harry Blacking. And there were two monks there - one in a wheel chair. We thought they could be the ones you saw at the monastery.'

'Very likely,' said Campbell. He'd spotted a file shaped bulge in her jacket and he was more interested in that.

'I'm sorry I put the phone down when you rang the office but the Chief was on the war path,' said Jenner. 'You know Tarnish; he'd want to hear what you'd called about. He'd say you were off duty and if you wanted to know about the case you should come back in.'

'Bottled essence of righteous anger,' said Campbell. "Perhaps," he thought, "Tarnish had attended the same management courses as that cockerel of a man from the laboratory – Stranfield, wasn't it?" Going back to his concern for his new detective constable, he added, 'I'd forgotten I'd told Flagg to check out Harry Blacking. He must have called on Renie Blacking. Because, of course, I then went to see her from the monastery. His nose must be a bit out of joint over it.'

'He'll live,' said Jenner at last sliding the beige folder from out of her jacket.

'The post mortem report?' asked Campbell.

'I couldn't copy it. You'll have to take a look at it while I'm here.'

Campbell watched her tightly folded blond hair as she went to look out of the window at the heavy mist coating the garden.

'Margaret will be back at lunch time,' he said, guiltily touching the file. 'She will expect you to have some soup with her.' He noticed Jenner's shoulders soften as he looked down at the contents of the smuggled folder. He knew Jenner would not give him away for working from his bed, but Margaret would know.

He scanned the pages up to the summary and there he slowed. He could trust the old police pathologist, Hemming, to do his job.

'It looks as though she was drowned then,' he said after a few minutes.

'Yes. In sea water.'

'She had some crowns on her teeth.'

'Yes. And there isn't a number in Geraldine's address book for a dentist either. Flagg, Garden and some of the team are visiting all the local dentists today.'

'She might not be Geraldine Franson.'

'Geraldine Franson never made her flight to Spain.'

'It still might not be her,' he insisted, arguing internally with the sadness that Jenner's words had dropped into his chest.

'The body's over thirty years of age, and so is Geraldine. And Hemming's done a sketch of the crowns – what's left of them. They're showing that to the dentists as well.'

'And there's always the people who make the dentures? What are they called? Orthodontic laboratories.'

'Of course,' said Jenner. 'I'd forgotten about them.'

Campbell returned to the post mortem's summary. 'Och no,' he said. He felt his frail insides flip over. 'Some of the cuts were made before death.'

'I know,' said Jenner. 'Now her death looks more like murder, doesn't it?'

'It might be and it might not be,' said Campbell. 'The pre-death cuts might still have been accidental.' He was angry with his illness for getting in the way. 'I'm sorry. I should have been at work. I should have seen this first.'

'It makes no difference,' said Jenner.

Campbell examined the rear view of his sergeant who refused to turn and face him. Her long pleated skirt quivered and the padded shoulders of her jacket pulled against the curve of her body as she hunched over the windowsill. Her reaction belied her words. The cuts to the corpse, made before the female had died, had been deep, ferocious and made with a sharp blade, the report had told him. He knew how much Jenner liked to be in charge of herself and the thought of such a violent action against a human life sickened him and, clearly, upset her. To help her self-control he said sharply, 'You're blocking my light.'

She swung round. 'Put your bed side lamp on then.' Her face was pale but tearless.

'So what else have you got for me?' he asked.

'A photocopy of the address book. Garden went through and phoned everybody. Nobody's seen or heard from Geraldine since the day she was meant to go on her holiday.' Jenner placed a bundle of papers, unevenly held together with a bull-dog clip, on the bed. 'The numbers where there was no answer she marked with a red dot sticker. Because of being copied they look like black dots. I'm sorry if they're a bit askew. Garden didn't have much time.'

'Och, that's fine.'

'Flagg was looking at Geraldine's diary so I couldn't get that.'

'Checking this list will give me something to do,' said Campbell. 'By the way, what happened about Lara Elves's story?'

Jenner frowned. 'We've checked the docks. No-one there saw the boat. She says that's because the tides were wrong. I think she might be one of these people that feel they have to have something important to say, and when they haven't, make it up. '

'Perhaps,' said Campbell. 'We might know more in a couple of weeks when people have had a chance to come forward with information.'

He flopped back on his pillows. Antibiotics seemed to be flooding into his blood stream drowning his ability to stay awake.

'And there's one other thing you ought to know...' said Jenner, causing him to open his eyes wide.

'Aye?' he replied.

'It's about Jack Wren...'

'He's not dead?'

'No...'

'Well then?'

'The garage where you saved him? The house belongs to Geraldine's mother, Mrs Agatha Spier.'

'I found,' said Campbell, 'an empty padded box and a pair of tweezers in the garage. They fell out of the car when I pulled out Jack Wren. I bagged them and left them in the back of my car. Perhaps you could take them back into the office. They could have held jewellery. Were any necklaces, bracelets, anything like that found in the garage?' He was relieved to be able to ask her this after his pneumonia on Friday night had made him fade away before he could sort it out.

'Nothing like that, but Mrs Agatha Spier is a jeweller. I've taken the odd thing to her for mending myself.' Her words explained her frown at him on Friday night. She'd expected to be asked about Agatha Spier and was confused when he had brushed her aside. 'I would have told you on Friday, Sir, but you really didn't look well. Do you suspect something was stolen from the garage then?'

'No,' said Campbell hanging onto the word with his Edinburgh accent. 'I told you on Friday the key to the garage was on the inside when I broke in. I think the box and tweezers were there because of her work.' He used his Celtic inner strength to push the effects of the antibiotics away for a little longer. 'So has Mrs Agatha Spier returned home yet?

'She's still away. As luck would have it she booked with the same travel agent Geraldine had booked with. We got them to check her details. She's on safari in Africa and no-one's been able to reach her.'

'What could we tell her?' asked Campbell.

'Her daughter's missing.'

'We can't find her, that's different.'

'We could ask her about the crowns on her teeth.'

'She might not know. We could be worrying her quite unduly.'

'Her daughter might have changed her plans and gone with her.'

'Yes,' conceded Campbell. 'Africa was on Geraldine's itinerary. She could have decided to give Spain a miss.' He heard Jenner sigh. Yes, he agreed with her: lying in bed made him argumentative.

Gravel on the front drive crunched and an engine revved.

'Quick,' he said. 'It's Margaret. Go down and stop her coming up. Hide this.' He passed her the post mortem report which she returned to the inside of her jacket as she left the room. 'And, Jenner, ask DC Garden to call. She was looking up details about the monks, Brother Joshua and Brother Michael.'

Jenner nodded and left.

The women's voices muted by the ancient timbers of the cottage soothed him. He felt tired and lay back on his stack of pillows. He pulled the clip of photocopied telephone numbers under the quilt and understood the part of his fever-dream about the vast quantity of soil coming from what seemed to be a small hole: you don't have to dig deep to find a wealth of information. The problem was the sorting of it and deciding what could be used and what could not.

'Now where,' he asked himself feeling the antibiotics creeping up on him again, 'should I start with these numbers in Geraldine's address book, at A and work forward, or Z and work back?'

Carroll Enderby channelled her gaze to the wall and the picture of the lady in a field of summer poppies. It was better than looking at the grey windy Monday outside or around the motor-way cafeteria, which only risked eye-contact with others. And that might encourage an approach. She looked at the poppy-lady's rounded figure and became aware of her own small bony frame. The distance she'd put between herself and St John's Town had helped her fear. She wondered if such a thing could be measured like a wave of light or sound. Or whether fear was more particulate in nature and could spread itself invisibly over tables and chairs and cars. It seemed possible because the note from the church almost hurt her fingers when she touched it. It hadn't been the promise of money she'd hoped for.

Geraldine had booked her on this course months ago. And the thought of Geraldine made her long for her now. Carroll wished she'd never phoned the number which she'd found in the suppliers file at the laboratory. It had so clearly belonged to Geraldine. It hadn't been hers to take. Perhaps while she was on this two day course Geraldine would come safely home or send a post-card from Spain or Africa. But this evil paper passed to her in a sacred place must surely mean Geraldine was dead.

At least, Carroll hoped, the blond, pale-green eyed policeman would not have followed her over a hundred miles to this cafeteria with its shiny plastic laminated tables. He frightened her, but then so did that strange penetrating stare of the Scottish Inspector. It had reminded her that she was already guilty of spying on her employer. And how she'd felt that guilt when Inspector Campbell'd spoken of the body on Catstail Sand Bank. She remembered his enquiring look when she'd assumed the body to be Geraldine's. No, she couldn't go to the police with her note. She could not explain to them why she'd made that first phone call let alone why she'd then gone on to a rendezvous at the church.

She pulled her crumpled unholy note from her pocket and spread it out on the table. She read it through to herself,

'The tongue also is a fire, a world of evil among the parts of the body. It corrupts the whole person, sets the whole course of his life on fire and is itself set on fire by hell.'

Her intestines seemed to have formed a knot preventing her diaphragm from moving. And for a moment she thought she might die. Then she thought she might never go back to St John's Town, the laboratory or the Wash.

'Have you finished?' asked a woman in a blue striped uniform, taking Carroll's cup.

'Yes,' she said, retrieving the hated note before it joined the crumpled serviettes in a heap on the waitress's tray. She daren't let anyone else see it. They would think her weird and send for the police.

The course registration was in an hour and Stranfield would phone the tutor to check she was there. And despite the risk she'd already taken with her job she didn't want to give him any excuse for taking anything off her salary.

Geraldine's instructions were so much clearer to Carroll than the map the college had sent her. But then, thought Carroll, they should be – Geraldine had been a student here. She looked up at the sign, "Saint Conrad House, Newington University." Geraldine had said that it used to house a small poetry department that had lost funding this year. The science department had taken it over and were running courses so that it could charge industry and this would help fund the whole department. In a moment of unusual chattering over a coffee break Geraldine had even told her that one of her old tutors was running the course.

"Say 'hello' to old Roger Rick for me, Carroll," she'd said.

Carroll wondered what she could say now to Professor Roger Rick.

The blocks of grey stone forming the walls of Saint Conrad House looked to be of stout Victorian construction. Carroll wanted a house probably not quite as big as this once substantial family residence, but not far off. People respected you if you had a house like this, she remarked to herself. No-one respected poor people.

There were two tables in the marbled foyer. One had keys and a navy suited smiling blond. Carroll wondered which factory turned out these people. They were too perfect to be flesh and blood. She also wondered briefly whether the girl would feel like plastic if she pinched her. But then her need to be registered on time caught her attention so she gave her name quickly to the girl and got her room key. Because of the hot air being blasted from a fan heater above her she became sweaty, so she removed her coat as she went over to the second table. A plump bearded professor with charcoal coloured skin, who was clearly more used to gabbling technicalities than manoeuvring people, gazed at his list and then at his pile of bound lecture notes as three of his new two-day students left the table. Carroll wished she could join in their chatter, but she couldn't. She could only think of the tangle of events surrounding her, controlling her. Careless laughter was for other folk.

She blinked. The thought patterns in her mind were flicking about like the fallen oak leaves caught by the gusting wind outside. Suddenly she wanted to be free of the burden of worry for Geraldine's well-being. She wanted to off-load it onto someone else. It was the only way she could sort her thoughts out. This Roger Rick would be the person to approach for such help. He knew Geraldine, but he didn't know her. He would not concentrate on her but would focus on Geraldine.

It wasn't until the academic volunteered to put her name badge on her lapel that she brought her mind back into the activities of the foyer and read his.

'Professor Roger Rick,' she said looking at his bright eyes and gleaming hair and beard, both frosted by grey.

'Indeed,' he said in perfect Oxbridge tones.

'I knew Geraldine Franson.' Using the past tense came so easily to Carroll it scared her.

'Indeed? I knew her too.'

'She said.' Carroll had no trouble keeping her voice steady.

'Lovingly, I hope.'

'Matter-of-factly.'

'Oh,' he said.

Carroll watched his bright eyes fade.

'Is she well?' he asked.

'I don't know.' She wondered if her face gave away the fear and sadness she wanted to hide but she still managed to control her vocal chords.

'What's wrong?' he asked.

'Am I the last?' she said pointing at the register of names on the table.

'Yes,' he said. 'Do you want to talk?'

His eyes invited her. Here was the stranger she needed. His soft voice destroyed the coating of normality she'd tried to cover her anxieties with.

'I don't know if I should.' An unwanted tear refused to stop in her tear duct and her words were cracked mid-sentence by the tightness in her throat.

'I think you ought,' said Roger Rick.

Carroll thanked him for the snowy white handkerchief he gave her and followed him. He said he knew a place they could go. There was comfort in talking to a stranger but she knew she would guard against telling all. She would tell him enough to let the pressure off, maybe tell him a few fibs – something close to the truth, but not as painful as the truth.

He cornered a table in a timbered tea shop. She couldn't remember the last time she'd seen such unguarded kindness in a man. She hardly noticed that his dark skin faded from her awareness as she absorbed his gentleness.

The words came out in a rush. She hadn't meant to be like this, throwing her worries at him. She knew she should have waited, got to know him – tomorrow would have been so much better. Carroll knew she ought to feel embarrassment but her mental load seemed to lighten with each sentence. She was startled to find that he knew about the body on Catstail Sand Bank. But of course, it had made the national news. But he didn't know about the enquiries into Geraldine Franson's life – they had not been broadcast.

When the waiter brought the coffee she leant back in her dark wood chair and studied the shortbread fingers laid in the shape of a starfish on the doylied plate. What more dare she say?

'Geraldine had a lover,' said Roger Rick.

'You?' asked Carroll. Geraldine had never seemed the sort to have a lover. Carroll had always thought Geraldine only capable of passion when it came to work. And this podgy professor wasn't Carroll's idea of a lover, but he was kind. And, perhaps, he'd appealed to Geraldine before ten years of good food had got to him. So she asked, 'When?'

'I was never Geraldine's lover,' he explained. 'The whole time she was at University here she only ever looked upon me as a friend. I wish I had been the chosen one. I told her I loved her once. I whispered it in her ear in the laboratory but she pretended she hadn't heard.'

'Perhaps she hadn't.' Carroll was relieved to look at someone else's problems instead of her own – even those of a professor in this provincial university who seemed to circle around his little world examining every pebble of his gold fish bowl time and time again. She found herself laying her tiny white hand over his.

'You're so much like her,' he said.

'I'm ten years younger.' Carroll felt the shift of control of the conversation leave the middle ground of the table and slip towards the professor's seat, but her voice remained even.

'That's how I remember her,' said Roger Rick. 'She sometimes used to wear sunglasses in tutorials. I'm sure her boyfriend used to hit her.'

Carroll realised that one of the shortbread fingers had been turned into crumbs on his plate by the hand that was not secured under hers.

'Surely that was all a long time ago?' she asked trying to neutralise his words.

'Yes, it was.' Roger Rick went to take another piece of shortbread.

She took it from him and put it back on the plate fearing the curiosity of the waitress at Roger Rick's destruction.

'Except,' he continued, 'She would phone me from time to time – mostly when she wanted to know something. She phoned me three weeks ago and I haven't heard from her since. Not that that is unusual, it was what she said that worried me.'

'What did she say?'

'She said she'd found her old lover. I said about his violence and she got really angry. She said he had become religious.'

'What's his name?' asked Carroll. She slid her hand away from his. She could feel his jealousy for Geraldine's lover. Despite the years since Geraldine had been around him it was eating him up. And she was sure it was because he was too soft to throw it off. Carroll felt stirrings of anger prickling her skin: you couldn't afford to be like that, you had to be hard.

'His name is Joshua Alexander.' There was a trembling reverence in his voice. 'Do you know your Bible, Carroll?'

She shook her head. The terrible phrases she'd been given over the phone and in her note scared her. She was sure they'd come from the Bible, but she knew nothing about its text. But she couldn't think of a way to tell Roger Rick about them without disclosing the criminal nature of the phone call she'd made, so she gave herself up to his story.

'The Old Testament is full of bold and angry acts. Joshua led the Israelites after Moses died. And with the Arc of the Covenant before him the river Jordan opened up as the Red Sea had done for Moses.'

'What do you mean?' asked Carroll.

'Joshua was a very powerful man. He took the city of Jericho. Once the walls were flattened by noise and vibration the city was destroyed, everyone was put to the sword except the harlot, Rahab, and her family who had let Joshua's spies into Jericho.' Roger Rick took a sip of coffee. 'Geraldine's man has his name and the same drive. I knew Joshua Alexander when he was a science student here.'

'And I suppose you're telling me Geraldine is his Rahab,' Carroll scoffed. 'Be realistic, Roger, Joshua Alexander has absolutely nothing to do with a character out of the Bible. I think it is you who are confused. Your jealousy has perverted a Bible story into a complete personality for a human being living in the present day.'

'You don't know this man.'

'You have wallowed in self-pity and it has brought you to this.' Carroll got up.

'Don't go.'

'Why? Because I'm so much like her?' Anger made her toes and fingers tense. The crackle in her voice hardened to shards of glass. He hadn't wanted to listen to her; all he'd wanted was for her to listen to his tale. His kindness had been a trap as clinging as her fear of being cornered by that pale green eyed policeman back in St John's Town. No wonder Geraldine had opted for the strong personality of Joshua Alexander. And she knew that if she'd been given that choice she would have done the same.

Out in the street Carroll Enderby realised she'd lost the opportunity to ask Roger Rick about the Biblical quotations she'd received on the phone and in church. As the rush of blood ebbed into a normal flow she started to walk. And as she walked some of the details she'd been told started to mould with the events of the last few days and make some sort of sense.

Geraldine had clearly taken up with her old boyfriend, Joshua Alexander. The number she'd found in the suppliers file had been his. And the note from Stranfield might have been advising her against the relationship because it might interfere with her work. Then, Carroll guessed, when she'd phoned Joshua, thinking Geraldine was selling secrets to him, perhaps all Geraldine'd done was drop the file and not put the papers back in order. It didn't even have all the latest details of the chip in it.

Carroll had phoned the number on the slip (it had been local) and she'd asked the voice on the other end for money. Perhaps his words taken from the Bible – from where she did not know, but they'd sounded as bold and angry as the story of Joshua in the Old Testament – had been said to frighten her. This he then had followed up with a note in church. He was just religious. Her mind sifted through the people she'd seen in the church at the Remembrance Service until it settled on the large monk.

At last she knew where to find Geraldine. She knew where the monastery was. It was local gossip. People complained they lived for free. Some said their religion was an excuse for an easy life. Even she'd heard about the monks in the old look-out tower before finding the phone number. It all fitted. She would check it out. There would be no money in it for her, but surely this was the least she could do for Geraldine. And later, once she'd managed to find the details of the chip, there would be no difficulty in selling the secret of the chip herself. Yes, things could work out all right.

Carroll paced back to the tea shop and found Roger Rick still nursing a cup of coffee and the last piece of shortbread. She perched on the edge of her seat and hissed at him:

'Make sure I'm registered for each module of the course, Roger.'

'Why?'

'Because I'm going to do what you should've done. I'm going to talk to Joshua Alexander.'

Chapter 7

Campbell slithered his lids half open and peeped through stubbornly slow to focus eyes at a man with thinning hair wearing a tweed jacket and baggy cord trousers – all in various shades of brown. The man was looking in the top drawer of his oak chest.

He'd heard the footsteps and the slough of wood on wood as drawers were opened but had assumed it to be Margaret tidying. Slowly, as he'd become more wakeful, he'd realised the steps were too heavy and the movement of drawers too urgent for his wife. And, anyway, hadn't she gone to a local gallery this afternoon to hang one of her fabric sculptures?

The man shut the drawer and turned round. His gold-rimmed spectacles caught the low sun beaming over the leafless trees and through the dormer-window. Campbell remembered his request to his wife as she'd left not to lock the door in case he had any visitors. He wanted them to come straight up. As a policeman, he decided, he should have thought more about the uninvited.

As his eyes became clearer Campbell had to accept that he had only learnt from observing the man that his face was vaguely familiar. His first reaction of fury, he smothered quickly in case this was a member of the medical profession sent to see to his well-being. And, because of his recent temperature and antibiotics, he also half-wondered if this man was real. When the lean intruder looked as if he might be about to rummage in the bed-side cabinet, Campbell felt such activity whether imagined or not ought to be stopped so he barked in his sharpest Edinburgh accent, 'I know you, don't I?'

The man jumped. He had the look of someone who was nearly permanently on the verge of ill health, thought Campbell.

'I'm sorry,' said the man

'For disturbing me?'

'Inspector Campbell, I ...'

'Ah, my name. Perhaps I could have yours?'

'Browme. Derek Browme. Ouseland Chronicle.'

Campbell remembered the man: he'd been the reporter sent by the local paper to cover court cases on more than one occasion. He recalled that he had not been pleased by the results of his slanted style of journalism, more suited to the national tabloids than a local paper. And not only was the face familiar so was the name. Browme. Polly Browme with her strong rounded body and swaddled infant had been the one who'd found Jack Wren overcome by car-fumes in Mrs Agatha Spier's garage. Could she really be linked to this weasel of a man?

'So why are you here, in my room, in my chest of drawers?' asked Campbell.

'I wasn't. The drawer was open. I'm a tidy soul, I was just shutting it.'

Campbell let the lie go. Derek Browme was clearly after a story, something different, not the usual stuff to be found in the local press which was carefully fed to them by the police themselves. He recognised that special hunger because it was akin to his own. And if Derek Browme was after information about the body on the sandbank he wouldn't get it looking there.

'My wife, Polly,' continued Derek Browme, 'told me how wonderful you were saving Jack Wren. It would make a wonderful human interest story for the paper. I'm sure your bosses would be delighted at such coverage, so beneficial for the force.'

The thought of pleasing Tarnish with his bronze crown glowing with contained natural violence was completely alien to Campbell. Feeling his temperature rise he said, 'Get out,' to Derek Browme with all the calmness he could muster.

'I could get the photographer to take a picture of my wife and yourself by the bed of Jack Wren.'

Campbell wondered if his condition really was having an effect on his mind. There was a curious sense of unreality about the situation. He decided to deal with Derek Browme by removing him from his room or his mind, whichever accepted his demand of, 'Get out.'

'The public have a right to know.'

'Ask your wife. Get out.'

Derek Browme unfortunately remained solidly human in front of him.

'All right then,' said Derek Browme, 'if you don't want to be the hero, you could give me the low down on the body on Catstail Sand Bank.'

'I'm off sick. If you don't get out now I shall arrest you for breaking and entering.'

'I didn't break in,' said Derek Browme.

'Trespass,' said Campbell. 'Out.'

The bedroom door swung open and DC Sally Garden's neat face, framed by a few fuzzy brown curls escaping from her pony tail, appeared in the gap.

'Can I help?' she asked.

Campbell hoped she could see Derek Browme as well as he could because he realised how much noise he must've been making – so much that he hadn't heard Garden coming up the stairs.

'What's he doing here?' she asked to Campbell's relief.

'Please see this gentleman of the press off my premises, Detective Constable,' said Campbell resting on his pillows. He had no intention of arresting Derek Browme: the press could be used in the same way pigs could be used for hunting truffles.

The exchange had exhausted him. The self-doubt had alarmed and wearied him. But he had so much to ask DC Garden after she'd escorted Browme out that he would have to gather all his Celtic strength.

'You'll wish you hadn't done this, Campbell,' said Browme as he left the room with Garden holding his elbow.

Campbell lay still listening to the descending feet, then the crunch of gravel as Browme departed and, finally, to Garden returning. He perked up at the thought of getting more illicit information about the body on Catstail Sand Bank. He knew he could solve this problem quicker than Tarnish or any replacement his boss could find – even with his illness dragging him down. So, by the time Garden returned to his room he was sitting upright.

As she entered, with her face blushing, he directed her to a hard chair in the corner of the room painted by Margaret with woodland flowers and birds.

'How have you got on with the sand bank woman's teeth?' he asked.

'We got nothing,' said Garden. 'Not one of the dentists claimed the work. One suggested it might have been done abroad. I don't see why we had to tramp round to each one in this day of fax machines and e-mails.'

'People ignore bits of paper and e-mails don't get opened, Garden. They can't ignore a pair of flat feet stuck to their carpet.' Campbell spotted her looking down at her small feet hiding in chunky flat shoes. 'Talking of bits of paper,' he said changing the subject, 'I can't read some of the photocopies you made of Geraldine Franson's address book. I've checked most of the numbers you couldn't get through to with the telephone company and they've all long since moved away. As she hasn't updated those numbers I think we can put them on one side. But, look, these two pages are not fully copied because the sheet was not straight on the machine.' He pulled out the bull-clipped wodge from under his pillow. 'Arthur F.R.A. That could be the start of Franson.'

'Yes, I remember that one. It is Franson. Because it was local I thought it might be a close relative so I asked a PC to call round. The house was occupied by different people and they've been there a couple of years. There was no forwarding address for Arthur Franson.'

'O.K. I'll look into that,' said Campbell. 'And this,' he continued waving a page, 'is Rog somebody and the phone number and address are completely missing off the bottom. As the entry is under R presumably that's what his surname begins with, but then again it might not if she keeps her address book like my daughter's – she puts them under the first letter for their Christian name.'

'I'll look at the original and let you know,' said Garden.

'And what about the monks?' he said moving quickly on to the next item in his carefully made mental list. 'You were going to look into their story for me.'

'Have you dreamed about them?' asked Garden.

Campbell looked at her long and hard. Was she going to pull his leg about the importance he placed on dreams? After all, he'd spoken about them to her before and she'd been as interested as himself. But, perhaps, with the passing of time she might have changed her views and just might be looking for cheap entertainment. He also reflected on the nature of his dream about the monks and their sexual rolling about on the sea wall. He certainly didn't feel at ease enough with DC Garden to tell her that so he answered, 'No.'

Garden's blush was renewed.

'So tell me about their trip to London,' said Campbell.

'I spoke to the registrar at the conference. He checked the seminars. Attendees have to sign in to each one. There are one or two quite big gaps.' Garden pulled out a sheet of blue paper. 'Brother Michael missed all day on October 31st and Brother Joshua missed the morning and the evening of the 31st – though he was there in the afternoon. And they both missed the morning of the 1st November.'

'London,' said Campbell, 'is barely two hours from here. They could easily have returned to their monastery on the evening of the 31st October and got back to the conference by the next morning. Come to that they could've returned during the night on any of the days.'

'I think during the night would be very doubtful, Sir,' said Garden again examining her shoes. 'I checked: neither Joshua Alexander nor Michael Ridgeway have driving licenses and the last train at night leaves at nine from London and the first train in the morning back to the city leaves at 6 am.'

'Thank you, Garden.' Campbell had difficulty keeping the irritation out of his voice. He really ought to be able to second guess these things before Garden said them. But she had checked without being asked and that must be a result of his training. 'You and Jenner had better go and see what those two monks were up to on the 31st October and the 1st November.'

'Yes, Sir. But I might not be able to manage it today. Tarnish has been giving me jobs.'

'What jobs?'

'Putting all the data on the computer.'

Campbell closed his eyes. 'Today, Garden, make sure you go today. That woman may have died from drowning, but some of her injuries were made before death. You must realise, Detective Constable, she may have been murdered by these people.'

Carroll Enderby looked at the car in front. The yellow street lights mirrored hazily from the backs of buses and cars as she thrashed her way through the evening traffic around St John's Town.

A couple of turns took her over the suspension bridge, past the new road and out onto the fens. A stream of white car lights flashed past her as she followed another stream of red rear lights out to the villages. Houses came and went with curtains not yet shut against the cold windy night, and the only light in the street came from householders' yards.

Another turn, memorised earlier from a map, took her towards the wash and the houses soon thinned. The map had shown the look-out buildings perched on the inner seawall. She'd noted the indirect route to them supplied by roads compared to the much shorter distance from St John's Town measured with a ruler. Constructing roads on this unsettled ground would have been expensive and still was. This knowledge didn't stop the distance slowly sapping her resolve to speak to Joshua Alexander.

Pairs of lights beamed across the flat ocean of fields as tractors moved like ships in a strange formation. She knew that they would harvest sugar beet regardless of the amount of daylight supplied by nature at this time of year. But darkness made finding her way difficult. And she felt alone.

Surely, she thought, the police would have found out the same story as she'd stumbled across. Others must know that Joshua Alexander and Geraldine had been lovers. Perhaps she ought to speak to the police in case they hadn't found this out for themselves. Then they could go and speak to Joshua Alexander instead. But she knew as she thought it she would never go to the police while the green eyed officer stalked among them.

So what would she say to Joshua Alexander? What would she say to Geraldine, if she was there? She had to be there. But surely, if they were together he wouldn't have bothered to contact Carroll at the Remembrance Service let alone feel he had to correct her for her dishonesty. But then, from the words he used on the phone and in his note, it was clear that he must think her evil. She wasn't that. She wanted money and respect, she wasn't evil. Perhaps she could tell Joshua that.

The fierce wind buffeted her car and slammed a flurry of sleet against the windscreen. The wipers cleared it and showed a light at the top of the look-out tower beaconing out towards the wash. Carroll braced her thin body inside her thick padded jacket and cord trousers and made her way to the second door along the L-shaped set of buildings as it had an illuminated door bell.

She found herself face to face with the sagging cheeks and chin of a woman no taller than herself.

'I thought you was me husband, Harry, come to collect me,' said the woman in a local accent, fingering a bright chestnut curl above her forehead. 'Who might you be? The brothers didn't tell me they were expecting nobody. They like to know who's coming in advance. This in't an hotel, you know.'

'I'm Carroll Enderby,' she said to the woman supposing her to be the house keeper. 'I've come to see Joshua Alexander.'

'Brother Joshua?' Suspicion tinged the sharpness in the housekeeper's voice.

'Yes.' Carroll supposed he must be.

'He's out.' The housekeeper started to close the door.

'May I wait?' Her nerves made her voice crack mid-sentence.

'I'll ask.'

Carroll watched the housekeeper move down the hall and enter a room on the right, her broad back clothed in a ruby coloured cardigan. She could hear her speaking to someone as well as the click and whirr of a computer. This was followed by a similar but louder sound.

The housekeeper returned and this time Carroll noticed her slim ankles and tiny feet nestled in fluffy heeled slippers. Behind the housekeeper a wheelchair entered the corridor from the room with the computer. Carroll recognised it and its occupant as the same ones she'd seen at the Remembrance Service with the big monk.

"What have I taken on?" thought Carroll forcing her knees to remain straight. "Suppose Roger Rick was right and Brother Joshua is violent - I'm as good as on my own here." Those words on the phone and the note she'd been given in church had been full of anger. She recalled his size next to the man in front of her. If talking to him went wrong, she could only call the housekeeper or the crippled monk. And all they could do would be phone the police.

And how long would it take them to get out here? Of course, the housekeeper's husband, Harry, might help when he arrived.

"No," she told herself, "I'm being silly. If Geraldine is here she will tell them who I am. She will understand why I'm here. I'm worrying about nothing. At least if Brother Joshua isn't here at the moment I could ask this other Brother about her. There is no danger in that."

'I'm Brother Michael.' The monk offered her his withered hand. His mouth trembled at the corners and was lost inside his beard.

"Look at him," she thought. "Brother Joshua looks after this man. Violent people don't care for others. They only care about themselves. I should know. "

'Come this way,' said Brother Michael.

Carroll could hear the local accent in his voice. She found it soothing her as he lead her into a room opposite the one he'd come from. Meanwhile the housekeeper went through another door at the end.

'You mustn't mind Renie Blacking,' Brother Michael continued. 'Old Renie's my guard dog. I don't like strangers so she protects me.'

Carroll thought she recognised the name Renie Blacking, but she couldn't recall what the connection was by the time she found herself in a square sitting room. A mixture of old re-upholstered chairs and settees covered in identical blue flowered material were arranged in a line around the walls. In the centre a pine coffee table supported note paper, biros and a paper knife. She sat on the seat nearest the door.

'We use this room for the retreats we run,' said Brother Michael manoeuvring his chair with clicks and whirrs from its electric switch and motor to within a couple of inches of her legs.

She looked at him. His dark eyes were like beetles scurrying about once their rock has been lifted and daylight has shone upon them. She wanted to look away, but he was so close he filled up her view.

'You've come to see Brother Joshua?' he asked.

'Yes,' said Carroll.

'I don't think you have,' said Brother Michael. His local accent no longer sounded soothing to her. He'd turned his voice into a sharp tool.

'Well, perhaps you could tell me about Brother Joshua instead.' Carroll didn't want to ask him directly about Geraldine and she thought his line in replies odd. She put this down to his dislike of unscheduled visitors but hoped he might mention Geraldine while talking about his fellow monk.

'No, I'm not in a position to tell you anything about Brother Joshua. You are quite mistaken about his importance. You've come to see me.'

'What do you mean?' She realised she couldn't stand up from her chair without pulling herself up on Brother Michael's wheelchair because he was so close.

'I heard your voice in the corridor. I couldn't hear the words but I think I caught a slight break in your voice. I've heard that before.'

'I don't know what you mean. Please let me up.'

'You want money, don't you?' Brother Michael's voice boomed out from his crumpled rib cage.

Carroll's body involuntarily lurched as every muscle in her body tightened from fright. And, she realised that her phone call had indeed been to this address. But she hadn't spoken to Brother Joshua; she'd spoken to Brother Michael. She took a deep breath. This changed little. It meant that Brother Joshua was more likely to be sane and reasonable if the eccentric quotes came from Brother Michael. And if Brother Joshua was sane and reasonable then there was more likelihood that Geraldine would be somewhere near him, and safe.

'I was wrong, Brother Michael. It was all a mistake. Your number was phoned accidentally. It had nothing to do with you or Brother Joshua.' Her voice cracked in the middle of the last sentence. Of course the phone call hadn't been an accident, but she had to calm him. She thought about calling the housekeeper.

'"The axe is already at the root of the trees, and every tree that does not

71

produce good fruit will be cut down and thrown into the fire. The New Testament: Luke, chapter three, verse seven. Do you deny you asked for money?'

'No, but I did not mean to ask it of you.' Panic curled around her.

'Does it matter to God who you intended to ask? He knows all.'

Outside the sounds of a car and feet on gravel allowed Carroll to pause. Renie Blacking was leaving. She and her husband were already too far away to hear her shout. She gripped the fabric on the arm of the chair. What was so different now? She had always had to cope on her own. She could control this situation.

She chastised herself for feeling vulnerable with this enfeebled monk, and his apparent attachment to a higher force held her in check. She could not push him out the way.

'I haven't come to ask for your forgiveness. Wanting money and the respect that goes with it isn't evil,' she said. 'I came to see Brother Joshua.'

'Avarice is a deadly sin.'

'I'm not religious.' Carroll fought back the fear that was trying to choke her.

'Do you know why these sins are described as 'deadly'? Because they are destructive. You will surely bring hell upon yourself if you harbour avarice in your heart.'

'The phone call was a mistake. I know that now, but I don't see that it's up to you to judge me.'

'"The tongue is also a fire, a world of evil among the parts of the body."' Brother Michael's shouting became a tortured scream which bounced around the room.

These were the words on the note Carroll had received in church. They filled her again with cold horror – only destruction could be associated with them. Perhaps hidden in his feeble frame was a murderous strength and she was not ready to be a solitary sacrificial lamb. This thought brought her back to Geraldine. Looking at his face distorted by anger she could suddenly believe anything of him. She had to escape.

'"It corrupts the whole person, sets the whole course of his life on fire and is itself set on fire by Hell."'

She gripped the arms of the chair and straightened her elbows. At the same moment she pushed her hips back and pulled her legs up to squat on the seat. She worked out that from here she could spring to the door and get out quicker than Brother Michael could manoeuvre his wheelchair to block her.

But before she had a chance to move the door swung open and the huge dimensions of a monk who, Carroll guessed, could only be Brother Joshua, entered. He took a mighty stride across to Brother Michael and flicked his chair into reverse. Carroll stayed where she was despite the distance between her and Brother Michael growing in front of her. She wasn't sure whether Brother Joshua's arrival meant she was now safe, or not.

'This,' said Brother Michael, 'is the woman I've been telling you about. Her name I now know is Carroll Enderby. She is the one I left a note for in church at the Remembrance service. I thought it would be enough to keep her away from us, but, as you can see, it has failed.'

'If,' said Brother Joshua, 'I'd known you were going to leave a note I would have stopped you. You see how you've frightened this girl.'

'She is an un-Godly creature,' said Brother Michael, his voice starting to wheeze.

'Go and rest, Brother Michael,' said Joshua. He sounded to Carroll as if a huge voice was caged inside his chest and only a part of it was being released to say, 'Let me sort this out.'

Although his words were unsettling Joshua's reassuring tones reverberated through her slight frame. She let her legs sink down to the floor and she lowered herself back into her seat. She watched Brother Michael as he gave her one last look, full of despising, and left the room.

'I thought he might kill me,' she said.

'He isn't capable,' said Joshua.

And, believing him, she said, 'Perhaps I ought to go.'

'Perhaps you ought to explain yourself.'

Carroll wanted to leave. She'd been wrong to try to talk to Brother Michael about Brother Joshua, and now she feared this monk would be just as difficult. These people were so wrapped up in religion they could twist the events of the world around the texts they'd implanted in their brains. What would they know of Geraldine Franson? And before she could stop herself she'd asked the same question of Brother Joshua.

And he turned the question on her: what did she know? So she unburdened herself telling him about the body on Catstail Sand Bank and Geraldine's holiday, of how she worked with Geraldine and how she was missing and of her own encounter with Professor Roger Rick. But she didn't mention to Brother Joshua that Roger Rick thought Joshua to be violent. He didn't look violent squatting beside her chair. He seemed to be staring at the table in the middle of the room.

Brother Joshua rose. His robes whooshed by her as his explosion of activity delivered him to the other side of the room.

'You mean,' he said. 'The police think that the dead woman on the bank could be Geraldine Franson.' His vast frame folded into the chair beneath him as if someone had punched him in the stomach. 'They never said so to me.'

'Did they know you knew her?'

'No, of course not, but I shall have to tell them.'

'Is Geraldine here?' Carroll's curiosity was burning her. If there was a risk to herself by posing such a question she couldn't see what it could be. This giant of a man was almost crying, when he looked up his pale face and hands were clenched but still.

'No. I told the police the only women here were Renie Blacking and her daughter, Lara. Inspector Campbell spoke to Lara when he was here and, Renie tells me, two policemen have been to see her at different times. She gave one of them a right mouth full, so she said.

Carroll slid off her chair and went to the big monk. She knelt in front of him and looked up into his eyes shadowed by his bowed head. 'Tell me about Geraldine,' she said. 'I need to know.'

'I loved her but I was not alone in that. Geraldine's life at University was one of free love and, I'm afraid, frequent changes of partner. I have to say I felt differently to Geraldine on that matter and we parted company. I suppose I resolved my problem by becoming a monk. I find a celibate life suits me very well.'

'But Roger Rick said Geraldine had told him that she'd met an old boyfriend who'd turned religious. You must have seen her recently. You talk as if you haven't seen her for years.'

'What business is it of yours?' Some of that caged voice escaped the bars of his chest as he straightened.

Carroll leaned back on her heals. 'I love Geraldine. She feels like a sister to me. I wanted her to love me.'

'Everyone wants that. Geraldine can't love. Even sex was not love for her. It was an amusing way of passing the time.'

'I'm sure you're wrong about her,' said Carroll. 'I thought you might know where she is. I thought she might be here.'

'I haven't seen her. Perhaps she has another religious friend. Professor Roger Rick is inclined to weave data of his own invention into the fabric of life.'

Every effort at control was beginning to fail against her body's urge to tremble. Carroll took the pen and paper on the centre table.

'I don't want money off you. I made an error of judgment. Please phone me if Geraldine contacts you. It would put my mind at rest.' Then she wrote down her home number and copied down the one for Saint Conrad House, Newington University. 'You can contact me at this second number tomorrow after that I'll be at the top one,' she said. 'My mobile's always got a flat battery and there's so many blank spots I don't often bother with it.'

'You were brave to come alone,' said Brother Joshua. 'You ought to carry your phone,' he advised.

'I know I should. I had to come. For Geraldine,' said Carroll hearing Brother Michael once again working on the computer in the room opposite. 'I have to go. I'm not meant to be here. I'm sorry.' She watched Brother Joshua finger the paper knife as he read the numbers she'd left him.

'You would benefit from one of our retreats,' said Brother Joshua.

'Goodnight,' she said and went back out into the night hearing him call,

'I'll book you in for Sunday? We need to pray.' She turned and saw him smile. 'Consider your real needs.'

The mention of a day of the week connected to the name of the monks' house keeper, Mrs Blacking, triggered something in her mind. She fitted the housekeeper's name with that of her escort on Saturday like sticking a tail on a donkey, because she knew where it went, Blacking. Blacking was the name of her escort out on the Wash on Saturday to pick shellfish for the lab.

Chapter 8

DC Lawrence Flagg turned the key to Geraldine's flat over in his hand. His pale green eyes lifted to look at Geraldine's door. Caretaker Stock had given him the key. That man wore his job like a title, thought Flagg. The silly old duffer had even asked him where his friends were. Flagg had delighted in correcting him.

'Colleagues,' he'd said. "What did Stock know? Nothing. Nosey old codgers knew nothing," thought Flagg.

And now he had nothing on old Campbell. The envelope he'd taken from Geraldine's flat had been a waste of time – all it had contained was a scrap of dark straight hair. A love token, from her lover or ready to give to her lover. What good was that? Even the diary was a dead loss – all it had was "holiday" marked in big letters over the end of October and the beginning of November. And now Jenner had taken the book off him and put it with her other junk.

He had to find something else, some other piece of information, something that Campbell would need, and he knew where to look. And he didn't even have to dally at her flat. All he had to do was collect the storage device he'd slipped down the back of the desk drawers.

The key turned easily inside the lock and Flagg went straight to her desk. Before opening the drawer he looked up at the photographs lining her shelves and found himself being scrutinized by one of the occupants' paper faces. It was the thin bald chap with his medals and his poppy standing next to Geraldine Franson.

'Was it your hair in the envelope, old man?' he asked the picture. 'You could certainly do with some.' He sat back in her desk chair.

'I didn't see you at the Remembrance Service. Oh, yes, I went. I wasn't going to let that woman Jenner and her attachment, Garden, get all the glory for going. I saw that wretched girl I followed. We went through the town and out into the country onto the road where that lab your Geraldine

76

worked at. I couldn't believe that girl I stopped was there, in church on Sunday. She was trying to hide her face. How foolish when she was wearing a yellow coat while everyone else was in dark colours. She saw me too. You should have seen the fear on her face. Brilliant.' Flagg picked up the picture and turned it over. Written on the back was 'Dad and me' and a date of five years ago. He put it back.

'Dad, eh? I'm glad I never showed Jenner this picture. That would have been as good as giving Campbell the information directly. And it's bad enough with that Scotch idiot being a blessed hero for saving that other old man from car fumes. What a waste of time! He should have let him go. Now Tarnish keeps bleating about it. I thought Tarnish would have more sense.' He opened the drawer with one hand and collected the data storage stick he'd hidden during his last visit. He gave the photograph of Geraldine's father a poke with the middle finger of his other hand.

'Are you dead old man, like Geraldine? No-one can really believe she's alive. And I shall soon know all about her. It will be in here. And I've got it.'

Today, Tuesday, would be the last day he would have in bed, Campbell told himself as he listened to Jenner's distinctively light and even steps on the stairs. He was grateful to have, eventually, a decent copy of Roger Rick's entry in Geraldine's address book from Garden. Then he frowned: on questioning Garden she'd told him that she hadn't been back to the monks as Campbell had told her to do because Tarnish couldn't see the point in it.

'Despite their incomplete alibi,' she'd said, '"Monks don't kill." Tarnish told me.'

As soon as Jenner came in the bedroom door her first words were to say she'd been phoned early this morning by Brother Joshua. And he'd told her a tale about a professor, Roger Rick, who'd tutored Geraldine and himself at university. And when Jenner'd asked him how he knew the police were interested in Geraldine Franson he'd said that Carroll Enderby, the laboratory worker, had been to him after finding herself on a course with the same professor. Roger Rick had told her tales of love between Brother Joshua and Geraldine.

Campbell was drawn back to his dream. The two monks gripping each other and rolling on the sea bank had obviously been just a fevered fancy, a product of his prejudice – something to be discarded.

'This surely brings Brother Joshua under greater suspicion,' said Campbell.

'And Roger Rick,' said Jenner. 'Garden hadn't been able to get through to him at the University before because he'd been away for several weeks at about the same time the body on the sandbank must have gone into the sea. And I also took the opportunity to ask Brother Joshua about the morning and evening of the 31st of October and the following morning that he missed from the conference in London.'

'And?' asked Campbell obligingly.

'There was a computer exhibition on. He took Brother Michael there in the morning, came back for the afternoon session and then went back for Brother Michael at tea time. Brother Michael had worn himself out so Brother Joshua stayed with him all evening. The next morning there was a seminar on the New Testament. Brother Joshua wasn't interested so stayed in his room reading. I haven't had time to try and confirm his story, but I should be able to check some of the details with the hotel. And Brother Joshua said he hasn't seen Geraldine for years. Then he got very upset.'

'Do you believe him?' Campbell asked.

'He's very believable. But he said Professor Roger Rick was obsessed with Geraldine. He could've just been trying to lay blame elsewhere.'

'Isn't it unusual for lecturers to go away during term time?' asked Campbell.

'Well, yes. Now you come to mention it, it does seem strange.'

'I'll ask him about it.'

Campbell turned to Garden's newly photocopied page, dialled Newington University and asked for Roger Rick.

The phone was answered by a crisp voice who put him through to another extension – once he'd announced that he was from the police and that he wanted to speak to Roger Rick. A series of clicks made Campbell pull the receiver from his ear. Then the phone made a peculiar burring sound.

Muscles tensed across Campbell's face as if these noises were sending alarm bells off in his head. He didn't want to be phoning he wanted to be out talking to people, seeing their faces respond to his questions, their bodies move in confidence or secretiveness. And, people couldn't put the phone down on you when you stood in front of them.

'I'm going to Newington University,' said Campbell shuffling his legs out of bed. 'There is a limit, Jenner, to the amount of information I can get stuck in this cot. You can drive me.'

The wooden benches of the lecture theatre made Carroll Enderby acutely aware of the sharpness of her hip bones despite her coat folded underneath her. Her dark bobbed hair tangled in her fingers as she looked down at the lecturer. She'd ceased to hear him half an hour ago. Roger Rick had been around barely long enough to introduce the speaker, and she'd been relieved at the way he'd avoided looking at her. He hadn't so much as asked her about her visit to Joshua Alexander nor had he asked if Geraldine was there. But perhaps he knew where Geraldine was after all.

Joshua Alexander hadn't been the monster Roger Rick had said he was. And at least she'd managed to untangle herself from the nonsense of trying to sell the chip to Brother Michael. Though, his Biblical quotes still managed to send her flesh cloying and cold across her back.

She'd hoped this course would have relieved her from the trap of the body on the sand bank and distance her from St John's Town with its pale green eyed policeman. But the mess of Geraldine's life was here as well as at home. If only she could free herself of all this she knew she could then concentrate on making the money she wanted. Being honest and hard-working hadn't worked for her mother. She wondered if it could work for her.

Having blinked and stretched with the others when the slideshow was finished she watched the lecturer move to the side of the display boards and offer brochures to his audience. This was the signal for the students to slide along the benches and file out of the door at the bottom of the raked seats.

Ignoring the brochures she started to thread through the throng with her coat draped over her arm. Three deep in the crowd she felt her other arm being gripped and pulled. She stumbled only to find Roger Rick levering her up higher than was natural to walk.

'What have you been telling the police?' he hissed.

He'd drawn her so close she could feel his fat being moved by the pull of her body against him and the bristles of his beard against her forehead. She thought about dropping her coat. Someone would pick it up giving her an easy chance of removing herself from him. But he knew something of Geraldine. She was sure of it now. And she would find out what it was. She could play along with his game until it suited her to withdraw, so she let him take her out onto the back lawns of St Conrad House. Once there she shook herself from his grip, put on her coat and set off towards a spinney at the far right hand edge. She could hear his gasping breaths as he followed her.

'I haven't spoken to the police. I went to see Brother Joshua, Joshua Alexander.'

'Someone's spoken to the police,' he said.

'How do you know?' asked Carroll.

'They phoned me.'

'But you knew Geraldine,' said Carroll. 'They were bound to ask you about her eventually.'

'No, it's more than that.'

'Why should it be more than that?'

'You must tell me everything Joshua Alexander told you.' Roger Rick wiped a tear from his eye.

Carroll wasn't sure if it was expunged from emotion or because of the cold wind, which was stirring the nearly naked branches above them.

She decided she would tell him what Joshua had said. That would quieten him. Even if the monk had spoken to the police already it would have been to explain his own relationship with Geraldine. Surely Roger Rick had nothing to fear from Brother Joshua.

She remembered her last conversation with Roger Rick – his pathetically unrealistic attachment to Geraldine. She didn't fear him, she only despised him. Even the strength he'd used to catch her on the way out from the lecture theatre must have been spent by now. She seated herself on the stump of a felled tree and examined his face moistened by his tears. She shuffled her feet in the top layer of dead crisp leaves and felt the damp ones underneath. She knew he did not know where Geraldine was. If he did he would not be like this. But he knew something of Geraldine. She could see the guilt on his face. The same guilt she'd felt when Inspector Campbell had come to the laboratory to ask her and Stranfield about Geraldine. Weak people always feel guilt, someone had told her that. She looked away and back down at the leaves bristling in the wind until she felt herself being hoisted and pinned against the rough bark of a beach tree. She looked up and found it impossible to see beyond Roger Rick's face staring at her from just millimetres away.

'You know where Geraldine is,' he said pressing his large fingers around her throat.

'No, I don't.' She kicked him in the shin. He was stupid, she said to herself as she dodged out of his loosened hands, professor or not. No common sense. Would she have gone over to Brother Joshua's at night if she'd known where Geraldine was?

She could hear him getting further behind her as she galloped over the short wet grass, so she stopped and looked back.

'You know. I know you do,' he shouted to her.

Turning away she found her body bounced off a scratchy wool coat cladding a willowy dark haired man. A bony face with nut brown eyes looked down at her and nearly smiled as she felt her hair catch in one of his coat buttons. She recognised him.

'It's the lassie from the same lab Geraldine Franson works at sure enough. And who's this chasing after you?' said Campbell.

Carroll felt her hair being released from the coat button by strong careful fingers, as she told Inspector Campbell it was Roger Rick. Taking a step back she checked behind the Inspector for any sign of the pale green eyed policeman. Her whole body sighed when all she could see was a policewoman in a full skirted navy suit and with her blond hair pulled back into a pleat. She vaguely recognised her, but she couldn't think where she'd seen her.

But should she tell them about Roger Rick's attack on her? She found she could not. Secrecy had become a habit along with fear. She plunged her hands into her coat pockets against the cold as she watched Inspector Campbell walk away with Roger Rick. She glanced at the policewoman's face and found threads of solid duty binding her features into a steady stare following the retreating figures, and yet Carroll new she was really keeping an eye on her. She knew science wasn't up to measuring such a human quality.

'You attacked Carroll Enderby,' said Campbell looking at Roger Rick's profile. He didn't need to be told, he could see it in the professor's rounded features sagging with spent anger and Carroll Enderby's blotched neck. As he moved away with Roger Rick the sinking sun threw the professor's face into silhouette obliterating the subtle changes made by mood.

'No, I didn't,' said Roger Rick.

Campbell let the lie go. Carroll might say something to Jenner, but he doubted it. He moved round the other side of Roger Rick to examine his face lit by the last of the sun's rays.

'I haven't broken any British laws,' said Roger Rick.

'So whose laws have you broken?' asked Campbell. He noted that Roger

Rick's body had started to shake and his skin turn grey with cold.

'Nothing that you need worry about, Inspector. '

'Would you be worried if Geraldine Franson was dead?' asked Campbell.

'She can't be. '

'You know a body of a woman about Geraldine's age and description has been found on Catstail Sand Bank?' asked Campbell.

'I saw it on the news and Carroll Enderby told me you thought it was Geraldine.'

For a moment Campbell was back on the sand bank with the fierce wind and sun seeming to be driving into him, pushing his body apart, weakening it ready for the inrush of tide. No, he told himself firmly, chest infection. Campbell knew you could get angry about almost anything, but he had neither the strength or the desire to fight. Aggression made more barriers than it broke down.

'Your study would be warmer,' he said. 'I've come from my sick bed to see you.'   Immediately he could see that making himself sound unthreatening had the effect he wanted of calming the large professor. He could almost feel him opening towards him as they gained the comfort of a gas fire and two inhumanly shaped padded chairs in Roger Rick's study.

'Why can't she be dead?' asked Campbell.

'She's in Spain and Africa.'

'Did Carroll tell you?'

'She may have done, but I knew anyway.'

'How?'  All Campbell's Celtic curiosity was poured into that one word.

'You might as well know,' said Roger Rick. 'I asked her to go to Africa and I understood that she was going via Spain.'

'When did you last see her, Professor Rick?'

'Not since September.'

'Two months ago, are you sure?' asked Campbell.

'It was her birthday, Inspector. I've been out of the country for weeks. I'm only just back.'

'You were at home in West Africa?'

'Yes,' said Roger Rick who looked, to Campbell, no warmer than he'd done outside.

'The same country Geraldine Franson was to visit? The same country her mother is visiting?' asked Campbell.

'Yes.'

'Her mother is a jeweller.'

'I know. And you know that is why I asked them to go,' said Roger Rick. 'You have almost worked it out, I think, Inspector. But my business with Geraldine and her mother could not result in her death in this country. There are risks but they are in my homeland.'

'I have to be the judge of that, Professor Rick,' stated Campbell. Roger Rick's dark eyes turned to him at last. Campbell could see that this was the truth he was about to receive from Roger Rick.

'I asked Geraldine to do this because I thought the thrill of it would make her love me. She's the sort of person who craves excitement, money and danger. She is frightened of nothing. That was all. Of course that did not happen. I hoped. I always hoped.' Sadness filled his eyes and slumped his shoulders.

'What did you ask her to do?' asked Campbell.

'In my homeland I am a wealthy man. I thought if I were to bring my wealth to Britain I might be more attractive to Geraldine. But the rules in my country prevent me taking any money out. Geraldine said she would do it. She only wants money, Inspector, not love.' His voice again lamented her lack of fond feelings for him.

'So how was she doing it?' asked Campbell.

'This will be her second trip. Geraldine's mother, Agatha Spier, makes up cheap jewellery with artificial stones identical as possible to the real ones I have bought in my country. Geraldine travels across Spain and on to North Africa by boat taking the cheap jewellery with her. From there she flies to my homeland. In the meantime I go home and arrange the collection of the gems by her mother. I leave before Agatha Spier arrives. She collects the gems, meets with Geraldine and replaces the artificial jewels with real ones. And Geraldine brings them out. Apparently the same jewellery goes out as came in. They don't even come back here, I cash them in elsewhere.

'There is no reason to kill Geraldine at least not until she returns and, although she is late meeting with her mother, she will be there. Someone could have mistaken the artificial gems for real ones and tried to steal them from Geraldine en route.'

Campbell leaned forward enjoying the warmth from the gas fire but finding no support for his back in the chair. 'Or perhaps Geraldine felt she was not getting paid enough and you could have killed her after an argument. The tour company said that she never arrived for her flight to Spain.'

'The booking was a red herring. She doesn't use the flights she books.'

'So how does she travel?'

'I don't know. She keeps that a secret even from me.'

'That makes your weeks in Africa over the relevant period less believable,' said Campbell, raising an eyebrow.

'I can prove where I was while I was away,' said Roger Rick. 'You can see my passport. I'm a British citizen. It is stamped and I still have the stubs from my tickets. And you can cross reference them with the airlines easily enough.' He went to his desk and brought back the documents.

Looking at Roger Rick's ticket stubs and passport Campbell asked, 'You said Geraldine was late meeting her mother. Does that mean you can contact her?'

'No, Agatha Spier would be the only one I would normally hear from. I can't contact her, but she can phone me if she has to. She phoned and told me that Geraldine was late.'

'I could get hold of her by informing the authorities out there what she is up to. They will arrest her, impound your jewels and, no doubt, prevent you from any further financial transactions. I thus urge you to make sure I can speak to her soon.' Campbell passed him a business card. He hated the wretched things. They weren't a real means of communication. No emotion was passed between people, except embarrassment, along with the stiff card printed with the tedious but necessary facts about the bearer.

Campbell also knew he would have to hide Roger Rick's activities from Tarnish by feigning forgetfulness or his superior would notify the West African Authorities straight away. It was a bargaining tool he was reluctant to lose just yet.

He drew himself out of the chair. He suddenly felt a long way from the comfort of his bed and he knew by now Margaret would have found his message about returning to work. Somehow he'd chased this autumn leaf of information and, at the moment of catching it, found it to be cracked and dry and turning to dust in his hands. Geraldine was no nearer to being found, nor could anyone confirm that she was the body on Catstail Sand Bank.

On reaching the door he realised there was a chance that Roger Rick would know Jack Wren. And this man just might know why Jack Wren had attempted to take his own life so he asked him if he knew him.

'Yes,' he replied.

'When did you see him last?'

'At Agatha Spier's house back in September. You know, on Geraldine's Birthday. Jack Wren was distraught at finding that he'd missed Georgina Brightwood's funeral. She was Agatha Spier's mother, Geraldine's grandmother.'

'He tried to kill himself. Do you know if he was ill?'

'No, I don't,' said Roger Rick. 'Poor old man. He had nothing to live for. His wife had died over in Canada. He'd been back several times to visit Georgina Brightwood. He'd known her in the war. I think he would have happily spent his last years with her – and then he found she was dead.'

'And what would you do if you found out that Geraldine was dead?'

'The same, Inspector. I should take my life. But she's not dead. Your body can't be Geraldine's. She is on her way to meet her mother in West Africa. You will have to look elsewhere for your murderer and your victim.'

But he looked away as he said this and Campbell wondered how convinced the professor was of Geraldine's safety. As he opened the door he stretched his neck. He'd been wrong to think that what he'd learnt was just like a dry crumbled leaf. It wasn't like that at all: it took many leaves to make a tree. His pleasure at this slightly light headed thought was broken by the sight of Carroll Enderby running down the corridor towards him.

She pushed past him and leaned over Roger Rick.

'You were more involved with Geraldine than you told me, weren't you?' she demanded. 'You told me she only phoned you occasionally. Were you lovers?'

Campbell was reminded of the last time he'd seen her at the laboratory by the break in her voice. He leaned back against the door and spotted Jenner turning into the corridor at the far end. He waved to her not to hurry because he could learn far more from Carroll Enderby's outburst than from hours of questioning.

'She doesn't want me,' wailed Roger Rick. 'She only wants money.'

'No,' said Carroll Enderby. 'She's not like that. She's not. You're just saying that because she can't love you. Is that why you killed her?'

'I couldn't have killed her. You know I couldn't,' said Roger Rick. 'I love her. Nothing can change that.'

Carroll Enderby pulled back and looked at Campbell. He could see she was asking for confirmation of this statement. He found himself nodding at her. Like a gazelle in flight she left the room. Jenner had just reached the study door so Campbell said, 'Let her go,' as he watched Carroll Enderby flee the corridor. And he wondered what plans Geraldine Franson had made to leave St John's Town and England.

Chapter 9

Sitting on the quay Curran Elves looked up from the oily fuel filter. The work on his boat had lulled his mind until he no longer saw the body he'd found on Catstail Sand Bank on Friday when he closed his eyes. This had succeeded where alcohol had failed. He put down his fuel filter wiped his hands on a rag and then across his bandy legs clad in old jeans and boiler suit.

He couldn't see the laboratory from the fishing fleet though he knew it was there, down river, beyond the inlet cut to harbour the fishing boats. He could remember the laboratory boss standing over him outside the pub on Friday night. What had he wanted with him?

Lara'd been asleep when he got in. But when he'd looked at her pixie features he remembered the faceless body on the sand bank. He wouldn't talk to her about it. She wouldn't understand. She would despise his weakness. That was what happened when a woman no longer loved a man. He went back to his fuel filter.

The tide was out this morning and the tired hulls of fifty or more boats rested on the silt. No-one else was about and that was the way he liked it. Lara had given him breakfast before setting out to work at the monastery. She'd chatted endlessly about the children as if he wasn't there. He could have been anybody, he was sure. She was always telling stories. She was good at telling people what they wanted to hear. It had almost been a rehearsal for when she would see her mother. Renie. Curran didn't mind his mother-in-law, though he never had reason to talk to her. It was her old man, Harry Blacking, that was a wrong'un.

What was it Lara'd said on Saturday night? Curran couldn't remember, he'd been drunk all day. Something about his Grandmother, Charlotte. The old lady'd been upset. Harry had upset her? Curran Elves felt his gut knot like the nets suspended from the boats about him.

And, as if his thought had been some silent command, he saw Harry's old land-rover draw up against the quay. What had Harry done to his Grandmother? But Harry had done so much to her already, what further hurt could he manage?

He watched Harry slam the car door and walk through the tidal protection gate, which stood open, and along the quay towards him.

'What do you want?' Curran challenged his father-in-law.

'You know why I'm here.'

'You're worried about what I told the police?' Curran taunted.

'I'm not worried I just want to know.'

'I don't know a thing about your business and I don't want to know.' Curran wanted to spit at him. 'Your business killed my mother and my father.'

'That was all a long time ago. And everyone knows no-one killed your mother.'

'You told her my father fell overboard and was lost. But you said you'd seen his body float by at night and you hadn't been able to get it out of the water before it disappeared in the dark.'

'I didn't know she would walk out on the Wash after him, did I?' Harry Blacking wiped the back of his hand across his face.

'My grandmother told me all about it.'

'Old Charlotte's always been mad. She's been mad since her own husband drowned. Perhaps your family are cursed. The North Sea might take you all. Old Charlotte's certainly brought you up to be as mad as her.'

That was it. He remembered what Lara'd said on Saturday: showing Charlotte the pewter box had been her father's idea. Harry Blasted Blacking. The knots in Curran's gut sprang loose exploding energy into his legs and fists. He threw himself at Harry only to feel his father-in-law's strength and cruelty behind the end of a heavy rope the older man swung into his stomach. Harry Blacking hadn't changed.

'You and your father took Charlotte's husband. You took her son and her son's wife,' Curran gasped trying to let his legs, which were buckled underneath him, regain their strength. 'You left her to bring me up on her own.'

'The sea took them, not me. Mankind don't control it all. The sea, you know, can take what it wants. Your grandfather fell overboard when he was with my old dad just after the war. I was just a nipper.'

'He knew what your hero father, Bert, was up to, that's why he lost his life.'

'And your dad, Curran,' said Harry Blacking slowly, 'was up on deck fishing alone – casting his nets to see what was about. I was asleep below. He got tangled in his own fishing gear and got dragged over the side and down into the sea. The nets were caught up on the rigging. I couldn't see your dad. I cut the nets loose. I had to. Everything would have been at the bottom of the sea. How do you think I felt, later, when I saw his body float by?'

'That's what you'd like the authorities to think.'

'That's what they do think.'

'You carried on the filthy business from your old man. I know. But old Charlotte deserves to forget,' said Curran. 'Lara didn't know about the pewter box. It was my Dad's good luck charm. He didn't take it that day because you dragged him out in a hurry. You knew. And you told Lara to show it to the old woman.'

'You should talk to your wife more,' Harry sneered.

'Like you do? Tricking her into upsetting old Charlotte.' Curran's anger nearly choked him.

'She wanted something to show old Charlotte that she could remember.'

'She's your daughter and you upset her as well as Charlotte.' Curran felt his right fist clench and unclench next to his thigh.

'She's not my daughter while she's married to you.' Harry hurled the words as an insult but Curran found it liberating. He didn't want Lara connected to this man.

'Your business will kill someone else before long,' warned Curran, looking to end the exchange.

He felt the older man yank at the back of his boiler suit. Anger like flames flashed along his sinews. He swung round. But Harry Blacking had side stepped among the scattered ropes and discarded fishing gear. Then he heard him speak,

'You've got something of the dead girl's. I've been told. It would be easy to tell the police, you know.'

Curran located him standing by the red brick wash-block. 'I have nothing of hers,' Curran replied.

'A jewel. I've heard. It doesn't belong to you.'

'You know who the dead girl is, don't you?' asked Curran. 'Is it Geraldine Franson from the laboratory, like everyone thinks? You could fancy Geraldine Franson, couldn't you? You used to take her out on the Wash to collect shell-fish every month. I know that. Did she turn you down?'

Harry Blacking's equally small square body hurtled towards him. Curran ducked and wrapped his arms about his father-in-law's calves. The older man fell onto the concrete. When he looked up Curran could see the grazing on his hands from the hard ground.

'Or is it someone else?' asked Curran.

'I shall tell the police about the jewel,' said Harry Blacking taking his legs from Curran's grasp.

'I shall tell them about your business.'

'You do that,' said Harry Blacking.

But Curran guessed neither of them would be speaking to the police.


Campbell felt he'd been summoned by Stranfield to the laboratory, even though he hadn't. A late start had eased him into Wednesday but Tarnish had been without any empathy for a Scotsman full of antibiotics and a need to work. Campbell's family had ignored him. And he knew that his drive to find out about the body on Catstail Sand Bank was pushing him into this madness of ill health and activity.

Stranfield strutted around the outside of the blue fabric seats stroking his red beard while Campbell tried to ignore him and relax his stiff neck by stretching it over the back of his chair. Stranfield stopped and hovered over Campbell's head. Campbell hoped he found it an obstruction to his progress. He hoped this might be enough to make Stranfield say what he'd been brought here to listen to.

'This, Inspector, is in the strictest confidence,' said Stranfield.

Campbell returned his head to the vertical and looked steadily away from Stranfield.

'Of course, Inspector, I don't expect you to be loose tongued.' Stranfield's sharpness told Campbell that he thought differently but was keen to appear polite. 'I think Geraldine,' continued Stranfield, 'was stealing information about the chip we are working on.'

'What makes you think that?' asked Campbell accentuating the Edinburgh tones in his voice. He was annoyed with himself for allowing Stranfield to rudely wriggle out of his questioning when he'd been in his pre-pneumonic state. Not only that, but he'd failed to tell Jenner or Garden to question him when they'd visited. Then he told himself off. The body had been found on Friday and today was only Wednesday.

'My desk has been rifled,' said Stranfield. 'My computer records have been interfered with and files are in a mess.'

'Perhaps your assistant, Carroll Enderby, has been slap-dash with her work. Have you asked her about these problems?'

'Not yet,' said Stranfield. 'She's been on a course for a couple of days and now she's phoned in sick.'

'So there must be some other reason that has made you suspicious of Geraldine Franson?' asked Campbell.

'I didn't want her to take a three week holiday.'

'Surely she's allowed her holidays?' asked Campbell registering an increase of irritation in Stranfield's voice.

'There are only two fully fledged scientists here, Inspector. Work of this nature requires to be developed at speed. There are always competitors.'

'Did you argue with Geraldine about this?' Campbell at last turned to Stranfield and looked into his eyes for a moment. The scientist's pale skin flushed with blood. Campbell pretended to ignore his embarrassment and continued, 'Work places evolve a personality of their own. There is the jokey sort of place but the jokes can sometimes be cruel; or there is "the boss is an ogre" type atmosphere where the workers pull together to survive. And sometimes there is an emphasis on sex and sometimes on power.'

'I don't know what you mean, Inspector.'

'Every work environment has a plus side and a down side. Power seekers are so busy gathering anything of any use to themselves that they leave the rest in ignorance and unable to function effectively in their job. People become frustrated and end up looking for work elsewhere in my experience. And, when they've gone, the hoarder of knowledge moves up. But while this is all going on the amount of work achieved is reduced.' Campbell could see Flagg's arrangement of office furniture back at the police station in his mind and wondered if his attitude had given Jenner any difficulties while he'd been away.

'What riddle is this?' Stranfield leaned on the back of the chair opposite spreading his large hands over the top.

Campbell remembered the powerful grip of his handshake. He could also see that Stranfield was angry but concentrating on his line of questioning, so he asked: 'What was it like to work with Geraldine?'

'I'm sure Carroll Enderby will tell you...' Stranfield paused and Campbell realised how little Carroll Enderby had, in fact, told the police. 'We argued,' the scientist continued, 'about everything: which way the experiments should go, how the chip should be developed, and staffing levels. This is top secret work. The fewer people who know the details of it the better. That is the only way to protect information.'

'Did you tell Geraldine everything?'

'Yes, Inspector. She knew as much about this project as I did.'

'Knew?'

'I use the past tense, Inspector, because I believe she has taken the work further and not kept me informed of her progress.'

'What makes you think that?' Campbell leaned forward resting his elbows half way along his long narrow thigh bones.

'Because she'd stopped talking to me, giving me reports.'

'Have you known Geraldine long?' asked Campbell.

'Since University.'

'Did you study with her?'

'No, she worked at the company I was at during her holidays.'

'So, you knew her well?'

'Yes, Inspector, I knew her well.' Stranfield's sigh told Campbell their relationship had been a sexual one. 'And I knew she'd started lying to me about her work.'

Campbell leaned back and said, as if delivering a well-known scientific theory, 'You could have argued before she went on holiday. The argument could have become violent. You could have killed her?'

'She specialises in the biological side, I am more of an electronics man. We need to work together. It would be like me chopping off my right arm to do anything to lose Geraldine.'

Campbell felt Stranfield's gaze challenge him to call him a liar, but he could see the logic in Stranfield's argument. 'So if Geraldine Franson were to sell what she knows,' said Campbell. 'She would need to contact someone with similar skills to yourself?'

Stranfield made a single nod of his head thrusting his crown of red hair forward and back in agreement.

Leaving the dubious comfort of his seat Campbell made for the door.

'What are you going to do?' asked Stranfield, Campbell looked at him with a frown sufficient to tell Stranfield that it wasn't his business to know what a Detective Inspector was about to do.

Campbell found himself outside the top floor flat inhabited by the absent Geraldine Franson. He was gazing at the locked door when he heard behind him a man's voice say,

'It's another one.'

'Another what?' asked Campbell maintaining the door in his field of vision but moving so he could also see the owner of the voice. The police style cap and navy jacket informed Campbell that this was the caretaker.

'Policeperson,' replied the caretaker. 'I'm Mr Stock. I can let you in, if you want.'

'Yes, thank you,' said Campbell.

The door opened, thought Campbell, like a shellfish opening to feed. Only he was the one here to feed on the information in the flat.

'The last person to come checked her clothes and shoe size,' said Stock. 'They even went in the bathroom and fiddled about in there. That body they found is going to be Geraldine's, isn't it?'

'I don't know,' said Campbell leaving Stock at the thresh-hold. 'Would you mind just waiting there a moment?'

Campbell noted Mr Stock's pleasure at this request. This sort of person saw most of what went on. He knew he would be of great help.

Without moving from his position two paces inside the living room with his hands in his pockets Campbell looked around the room. He liked the solid wood furniture and the modern art. He didn't feel guilty at looking in this way. How she lived and what she liked were as important to his investigations as finger prints. Even so, he next focused on Geraldine's desk.

The computer was gone as was the diary, of course. He looked through the desk. He was sure something was missing. There would be some sort of information back-up. There was nothing of that nature here.

Campbell approached the table in the middle of the room and picked up Jenner's receipt of items taken from the flat. He glanced down it before returning to the desk. As he got nearer he moved his head lower to see how much dust had fallen on the area. Geraldine had been gone well over a week. He checked the drawers but couldn't find any software for the computer there or anywhere else. He tucked this information to one side and looked at the photographs on the shelf.

Lines free of dust showed they'd been moved around, but this Jenner had accounted for in her report of the initial search she carried out with Garden and Flagg. He spotted the picture Jenner had mentioned of Geraldine's mother, Mrs Agatha Spier, from her description of being plump and having blue tinted grey hair. He decided to take it with him in case he had to inform the West African authorities of her part in smuggling out Roger Rick's wealth. So he added it to the bottom of Jenner's receipt.

Those photographs looked out at him as if the people in them were trying to speak to him. They were Geraldine's back-ground. The people she loved. He found no pictures of men of her own age. There were no Stranfields or Roger Ricks. And what of Jack Wren? Perhaps he knew what had become of Geraldine. He was staying at her mother's house after all. But surely if what Roger Rick had told Campbell was true, that would not be enough to make Jack Wren want to kill himself. There was, of course, another possibility and that was: if Geraldine was the body on Catstail Sand Bank, then Jack Wren could have had something to do with her death. And many a person commits suicide after murder, but usually with the same weapon they killed with, and, usually, soon after the murder, not a week later.

Campbell just couldn't bring himself to believe that the fine boned, malt-white haired Canadian could have stabbed Geraldine and left her to drown. But he would have to be questioned if he regained consciousness. In the mean-time he could check to see if he had a close connection to Geraldine because, surely, there would be a picture of him among the photos.

He moved them about, but he could only find one of an older man. This one was bald with a wiry face and frame. He was wearing a heavy coat with a poppy and he was standing next to a long haired Geraldine similarly clad. On the back he read the inscription, 'Me and Dad,' and a date of five years ago.

Having picked it up he took it across to Stock, who was waiting like a faithful hound where he'd left him. If it wasn't for the fact that humans don't have tails, Campbell was sure the caretaker would have wagged his.

Before he was able to ask about the picture Stock told him about all the police visits. The second visit by the blond green eyed policeman stood out as one he'd not been told about. Campbell had no doubt it was Flagg who'd been in. There was nothing on the receipt signed off as taken by him. He hoped his detective constable's actions had been a mistake but somehow he doubted it.

Stock had plenty to say about the picture too. He confirmed that this man was Arthur Franson, Geraldine's father and, with no persuasion at all, he told Campbell that the old man lived in bed and breakfast accommodation on the outskirts of St John's Town.

Wondering how much time separated the births of Mr Stock and Mr Franson, Campbell left to interview Geraldine's father.

Carroll Enderby laid her driving license, log book and car insurance certificate on the police station's counter with the form the green eyed policeman had given her on Friday morning. She knew she'd phoned in sick, but it didn't matter. There was only Stranfield to worry about, and he would be down at the laboratory so no-one would see that she wasn't house-bound.

The fatherly face opposite her said, 'Good morning, I'm Sergeant Porter,' and brought out a small black folder from under the desk. She glanced over his shoulder into the clean cream office beyond furnished with old desks and chairs, and decorated only by maps of the area. It had taken all her nerve to get herself here and if that green-eyed policeman was lurking somewhere she didn't know whether she would be able to stand her ground.

'I can't find the copy,' said Sergeant Porter folding his shiny face into a frown.

'Oh?' said Carroll with the crack in her voice barely contained not knowing what this meant. But she was sure that the blond policeman with green-eyes would be called to assist.

'Who gave you this ticket?'

Carroll tried to explain as calmly as she could the policeman's square, even features although all she could think about were his intimidating green eyes and the bristling, nearly white fair hair.

'He was uniformed?' asked Sergeant Porter.

'Yes.' There was something wrong about the ticket she'd been issued. She could tell that from Sergeant Porter's reaction.

'Then he would have a number,' he said tapping his shoulder.

Carroll closed her eyes trying to cut out the police station. She placed herself back in her car down the road to the laboratory on Friday morning. She could see the blond, green eyed policeman coming towards her. He wasn't wearing an identification number on his uniform. Relief swam through her. He wasn't a policeman after all – just some odd character pretending to be one so he could use their powers.

Now she could tell them everything she knew about Geraldine, Brother Joshua and Roger Rick. The police could catch this intimidating police-posing creep.

'I work at the laboratory where Geraldine Franson worked,' she started.

'What number was the police constable wearing who gave you this ticket?' asked Sergeant Porter again deepening his frown. 'Ah, DC Flagg, perhaps you could help us.'

Smiling Carroll turned round to tell all to the person being addressed with reverence by the shiny faced policeman behind the counter. A detective constable would know about Geraldine Franson. She would get some sense out of him.

Her relief and pleasure turned to steel, her muscles flinched and her face moved back as if the blond haired, green-eyed policeman had struck her. The man who'd given her the ticket was a policeman. He was this policeman.

Gripping the edge of the desk she asked to see Detective Sergeant Jenner. She'd been so helpful yesterday in the garden of St Conrad's House when Inspector Campbell had gone off to talk with Roger Rick.

'Can't DC Flagg help you?'

She glanced at Flagg. Flagg hadn't been bearing his number on his uniform on Friday. Then he'd been at the Remembrance service in church on Sunday wearing that "I'll get you" look along with his Sunday best. And now he was here, a detective constable not even needing to be in uniform.

Then she wanted to unsay that she wanted to speak to DS Jenner. Because she'd tied together the memory of the kind Jenner from yesterday with the one of the woman who'd helped her in church at the Remembrance service. They were the same person. Jenner and this Flagg worked together. They must have been at the Remembrance service together. Carroll swore at herself. She had been so terrified by that stupid telephone call she'd made to Brother Michael and been too interested in making money out of it that she hadn't fully realised who was with whom.

She wanted to run but Flagg was between her and the door. She tried to read his face. It had a wary look.

'It's this ticket,' started Sergeant Porter.

'That has nothing to do with my work,' said Flagg.

He must have realised this would happen, thought Carroll. He issued the ticket. He must have known I would bring it in. His game has gone further than he reckoned it would. And so he must be playing it on his own.

'This young lady says she works at the lab where Geraldine Franson worked. Carroll Enderby?' Sergeant Porter read her name off the papers in front of him.

Carroll saw recognition register in Flagg's features. She knew then that he hadn't known who she was when he'd given her that ticket. Though he must have seen her name mentioned in reports since he wrote her name down on his note pad out on the laboratory road. Only his hormones, she decided, had blocked the connection.

So now he knew. And somehow that made him more dangerous. Though she didn't know why.

'I have to see Inspector Campbell,' she said turning back to the counter. She might not be able to trust Jenner because of her connection with Flagg, but a policeman of a higher rank should be able to help.

The thup of the front door of the police station swinging shut made Sergeant Porter look over her shoulder. She followed his gaze. Flagg was gone.

'Inspector Campbell's out,' said Sergeant Porter with a sigh.

She realised all he cared about was having his paperwork straight. He couldn't see that a crime had been committed. As far as he was concerned, he just couldn't read the signature and whoever gave her the ticket forgot to put his number in the right box.

'Now let's look at these papers,' Sergeant Porter continued. He muttered to himself like someone being given an extra job when he was already busy, 'He could have got this information from the computer.'

'You have the papers, all of them' said Carroll drawing her hands away from the reception desk. 'I don't want them.'

She turned and left. She wanted to walk briskly to her car among the people of St John's Town. Somehow she didn't think Flagg would be waiting for her. He'd obviously been startled by her wanting to speak to Inspector Campbell. He would be expecting her to be in the police station for hours. And he must have guessed she would tell the Scottish Inspector of his extra activities.

Lunch time cars crisscrossed her journey over the road in front of the police station. If only Inspector Campbell had been there, she thought. But he wasn't, so she would go back to work this afternoon and put up with Stranfield's bullying. After all, it was nothing compared to what she'd been brought up with.

Chapter 10

Campbell knocked on the open door below the grey 'B & B' sign. The afternoon had been marked by a drop in the wind and the loss of the sun behind an ivory sky. The air had become damp and this chilled Campbell's feet. As he moved up and down on his toes he breathed lightly to try to avoid a lung full of the crumpled old man beside him. The man stood on the front steps as if he was giving himself an airing or watching the weather.

'He's gone on holiday to Spain,' said Campbell's companion. Despite his efforts Campbell recoiled at the smell of rotting teeth. 'You can go on in, though,' continued the old man. 'He's got some help in temporary like.'

The dull paintwork of the door gave way to a yellowed interior. Campbell turned back.

'Are you coming in,' he asked the old man.

'No, I have to wait out here.'

In the front hall Campbell pressed the button marked, 'For attention,' and examined the geometric pattern showing through the dirty paint.

Beyond the stairs a small stout person moved in the shadows towards him. Closer, the light from the front door showed the sagging face, and bottle bright chestnut curls of Renie Blacking. He showed her his warrant card and introduced himself.

'I know you,' she said, 'and then you sent that Detective Constable Flagg. It takes two interviews and two different policemen to ask the same questions now, does it? "Where has your husband been for the last ten days? What's his job? What does it involve? Is there anything that gives you cause for concern?" Harry's a hero's son and like his father in every way. I told you that. I told that yellow-haired policeman. And I'm telling you again.'

Campbell knew he had to be fair. It was his job to listen with an open mind. Yet to him she sounded like a gull pulling at refuse and shrieking at her finds. Her complaint of over-zealous interviewing was useless after the passage of just a few days. Her argument was rubbish from the tip, not food, but this gull looked ready to fight over it. So he threw her the equivalent of a sandwich with, 'I've come to see Mr Franson.'

'What's Arthur done?' she asked spreading her body across the passageway.

Campbell wondered if she was defending Geraldine's father. 'He's here, then?' he asked.

'We have all sorts,' said Renie Blacking. 'Druggies, mental break downs. No-one else will take them. Mr Drinton, the owner, he looks after them. It's the least I can do to help when he's away. Mr Franson is an alcoholic. He was in prison before he came to us.'

Campbell felt he was undergoing a delaying tactic but couldn't resist a little lateral investigation, so he asked, 'How's Lara managing without you to look after the children.'

'She's been taking them with her to the monastery. I'm still doing evenings up there. The Brothers have got a retreat this Sunday, but Mr Drinton will be back by then.'

Campbell noted how relieved she was to talk and stay in the front hall, which led him to say, 'Could you show me to Arthur Franson now?' using his most authoritative Edinburgh tones.

A door opened behind her letting out the rattle of pots and pans being washed up. A bare bulb in the kitchen highlighted the grimy woodwork and greasy ceiling.

'Shut it,' screamed Renie Blacking rushing over to pull the door to. Campbell heard her hiss through the gap before closing it, 'He'll have the Health Inspector down on us.'

'I'm not interested in your domestic arrangements, Mrs Blacking,' said Campbell taking the first four stairs up. 'This way is it?'

Renie Blacking smiled at him. 'I wouldn't have it like this if I ran the place,' she said.

'I know,' said Campbell noting the rodent chewed and scratched woodwork on the stairs. He hoped she wouldn't.

She showed him to the third door on the left before returning to the ground floor. He knocked. There was no reply. He heard shuffling noises and muffled steps. Someone was standing the other side of the door.

'Mr Arthur Franson? Inspector Campbell, police, may I come in?'

'Indeed, indeed, come in,' said an old but refined voice from the other side.

When the door opened wide, Arthur Franson met Campbell's gaze with blue, blood shot, pasty eyes. His skin, Campbell noted, was so transparent it was tinged with purple. Arthur Franson was short but then so was Geraldine. He matched the image of the man in the photo next to Geraldine Franson, named 'Dad' on the reverse.

Franson sat on the thin mattressed bed and Campbell drew up the only chair next to him.

'I've come about your daughter, Geraldine, Mr Franson,' started Campbell.

'I haven't got a daughter,' said Arthur Franson.

'You were married to Agatha Spier?'

'No, Inspector. My brother, Herbert, was. We were twins. Now what can I tell you? Agatha Spier was Agatha Brightwood in our youth. She married my brother and became Agatha Franson and then she married that Reggy Spier some twenty years ago now. She said we were too old for her. She said we were nearly as old as her father.' Arthur Franson smiled. His mouth lacked some of its teeth and any replacements.

'And Herbert, where is he?'

'Dead. Heart attack last year. It couldn't take any more.'

Campbell felt as if someone had kicked him in the jaw. Geraldine's father had been taken away from him no sooner than he'd found him. And yet Arthur Franson spoke as if he'd somehow been part of his brother as even the very problem of Herbert's marriage he wanted to share by saying 'we'.

'You were nearly as old as Mr Brightwood?' said Campbell falling into Arthur's own thought pattern. He meant 'you' plural because he needed to know about Herbert, not Arthur.

'We were younger by just five years than Mr Brightwood. But was Herbert Geraldine's father? That's the question you ought to be asking yourself. She could have been Spier's child all along.' He paused, waiting for encouragement.

Campbell provided a fascinated, 'Oh.'

So Arthur continued, 'The story goes back further than that. History has a habit of repeating itself. To start with: who was Agatha's father? The story goes that old Mrs Georgina Brightwood – so recently dead, bless her – had an affair during the war with a Canadian, Jack Wren. He was rich. That was what old Georgina liked about him.' Arthur stopped plucking his blanket and looked casually under his thin pillow. 'I'm sorry. It's not polite to talk about money. Would you like a drink?'

'No thank you,' replied Campbell. 'I know it matters to you whether Geraldine was your brother's daughter, but, from her features in the photographs I've seen of her, it strikes me that there is a great family resemblance.'

'She has our blue eyes and our dark hair, when we had our hair, of course, and our build. I believe she very probably is my niece,' said Arthur pulling a bottle wrapped in brown paper from under his pillow. 'You don't mind if I partake.'

'Indeed not.'

'But Agatha Spier is a liar like her mother. A liar. Truth is a toy to her. Does anyone really know what these women get up to? You must be married. What do you think your wife is up to right now?'

With his look Campbell told him that he wasn't going to answer.

'I'm sorry, Inspector. My manners aren't what they were.' Arthur Franson plucked at the neck of the bottle with his thin lips. His fingers rustled the thin brown paper around it.

'You should see your face, Inspector. Don't be cross. I never bothered with women on a permanent basis myself. Knowing the truth about them is not an easy thing. A man in your profession must understand that.' Arthur's pale fingers flicked his blanket away from him.

'Your niece might be dead, Mr Franson,' said Campbell bringing his own mind and, hopefully, Arthur's back to the reason for him being here.

'So she might be, Inspector, and it's no surprise to me.' Arthur Franson sucked in his thin lips and rose from the bed.

'Would you be able to identify any of her clothing?' asked Campbell wondering if anyone could work anything out from the discoloured silk found on the body on Catstail Sandbank.

'No, Inspector. I only saw her occasionally.' Arthur Franson lowered his voice. 'She's topped up my funds from time to time. And on those occasions she's barely spoken to me.'

'Do you know anything about any dental work she may have had done?' Campbell asked trying to keep the lost hope from his Edinburgh tones.

'Of course I don't. Excuse me, Inspector. I have an appointment I have to keep. Goodbye.'

'Jack Wren has attempted suicide,' Campbell persisted.

'I never knew the man well myself,' said Arthur Franson holding the door open. 'Herbert knew him better than me.'

As Campbell loped down the stairs Irene Blacking came out of one of the rooms clutching a bundle of clothes. Her face reddened. 'Laundry,' she explained.

'What appointment has Arthur Franson got?' asked Campbell.

'The only appointment that man will have is with a bottle,' she replied.

Campbell noted that the man outside from earlier had shuffled down the street. Once in the car Campbell looked at the photo he'd taken from Geraldine's flat. The caretaker had thought he knew who and where this man was. He too had thought him to be Geraldine's father. False knowledge. Like one of Agatha Spier's gemstones. But like her Campbell'd replaced it with the real thing.

Staring at the details of Geraldine's father's face to try and detect the tiny differences in a twin's features, he noted that the size of the photograph wasn't standard so he removed the back. The picture unfolded to reveal the man Campbell had just seen standing next to Herbert Franson. On close comparison he could see Arthur had a heavier jaw and a squarer temple, but apart, without the chance for comparison, they would have looked the same to a stranger.

The photo wouldn't have been taken by Geraldine's mother – long since divorced from Herbert Franson and remarried to Spier. So some third party must've taken it. Campbell stretched his neck. The quality of the picture could have meant it was a professional job.

Campbell was about to phone the local newspaper when thoughts of Derek Browme, poking about his bedroom after a story, stopped him. Perhaps he would get Garden to check it out. After all, he couldn't describe such an activity as mainstream investigation. It could almost be described as idle curiosity. But he would still visit whoever the photographer turned out to be. He had to know everything he could about Geraldine Franson.

Carroll Enderby felt herself shake. All these bullying men had exhausted her and yet she had to stand here and take more.

'You've been at my files,' said Stranfield. His large hands were resting on two desks on either side of him: Carroll's and Geraldine's. His brogued feet were spread between the desks. His face leaned towards her. His pale skin and red beard caught the white light from above.

'It's my job,' said Carroll. From the seat behind her desk she felt very small.

'They're not in the right order.'

'I'm sorry. I'll do better.'

'You've been tampering with them.'

'I've looked at them, yes. But I didn't turn the contents round. Someone else did that.'

'There's only you, me and Geraldine.'

Carroll didn't want to blame Geraldine even though that seemed the only way to keep her job so she said, 'You and Geraldine were fighting before she went away.'

'That's none of your business.' He spat out the words and took a step towards her.

Carroll longed to have a witness to this. The same as when her father attacked her mother. But there had been a witness then, little Carroll. And she hadn't been able to help. All she'd been able to do was write each parent a note saying, 'Please don't fight'. And her father'd come to her and said, 'We're not fighting.' And little Carroll'd said, 'Please don't go.' And her voice'd cracked for the first time. And he'd said, 'I won't.' And then he'd gone. A witness to Stranfield's temper wouldn't help now.

Carroll looked up. Her own anger curled her lip across her teeth and narrowed her eyes. She could match him any day.

Stranfield rocked back to a more upright position. 'We were not fighting,' said Stranfield. 'We were having a difference of professional opinion.'

'You've always been jealous of her abilities. You put her down at every opportunity to make you feel better.'

'If you say one more word you're sacked.'

'And I'll do my explaining at the tribunal for unfair dismissal.' Her voice cracked in the middle of 'explaining'. She was livid. It made her sound so weak.

Stranfield turned away and Carroll wondered why he hadn't sacked her. She knew she deserved to lose her job. She'd taken information, the list of investors. She'd even tried to sell the chip to the monks. Oh. Hadn't Stranfield been standing near the monks at the memorial service? Hadn't Geraldine gone to University with Brother Joshua Alexander? And she knew Geraldine and Stranfield had known each other for a long time from the way they'd spoken to each other and the careless movement of their bodies whether working or fighting. Stranfield must know the monks. Then she sighed because they hadn't told him of her visit when she was meant to be on her course or he would have sacked her already.

'You'd better do your job properly in future,' said Stranfield. 'And you'd better go out on the sand banks on Saturday for the mussels and cockles. Here.' He gave her a piece of paper.

Carroll looked at it: a written instruction.

'I shall consider it a breach of your contract of employment if you fail to go.'

She wanted to refuse, like she'd wanted to tell someone about her father. But she hadn't then and she wouldn't now. The job was all she had, but if she could find the research on the chip she could sell that.

Clenching her teeth, Carroll realised her bitterness was trying to pervert her back into sly theft. Brother Joshua was right. She needed to take a day out. He had proved trustworthy; he had kept her counsel. She'd phone him and go to the retreat on Sunday.

Lawrence Flagg kicked the wheel of his car fitted out in police trim.

'Stupid fat git. Sergeant Porter didn't have to say anything about the ticket.'

No sleep, all night. Three o'clock by the garage clock. Still dark. Still safe.

He pulled a paint brush and a tin of red oxide from the racking lining his garage and started to daub the paint over the white and orange body work.

'All Porter had to do was take a note of her documents. No-one would have known. Now I'm going to be caught.'

He painted out the swear words he'd written across the car.

'The first girl I'd stopped too – following the others had been enough – and she has to screw it right up.'

He shook a lidded can of petrol at the car.

'I'll have to torch you because of Carroll Enderby. I did everything right. I waited for a lonely spot, down that road to the laboratory.'

Flagg put the can down. The laboratory. Of course. Geraldine Franson. He hadn't time for this now. He had Geraldine's computer files sitting by his own machine.

Slinging the paint brush at the car he flung open the garage door and took four steps at a time to his living room. His sweaty palms caught on the data storage device. He could feel the power of having such a thing in his hands. It stiffened his fingers and traced along his arm muscles to catch his shoulders and push up into his neck and jaw. He didn't want to swallow the name of the person he'd beaten by finding this information so it spilled out of his mouth, 'Campbell.'

Thursday's dawn caught Flagg's eyes. He yanked the cable. The computer plug sprang out of the socket. The screen died.

'Nothing but a file name,' screamed Flagg. 'All's useless.' He pulled the storage device from the computer onto the floor. And cried. He crumpled down to sit beside it.

'I hate,' he said. 'I hate. I hate.' He stamped on the storage device breaking the plastic cover. 'I can't be a policeman. I can't go back there. It's all Carroll Enderby's fault I don't have a job. She'll have told them by now about my car and my uniform. And she'll still have her job at the lab.' Flagg fingered the remains of the device. He rubbed his fist across his face.

'The same lab as Geraldine Franson.' Flagg traced a line over the carpet with a felt pen. Last Friday following Carroll Enderby through the town had thrilled him. Then she'd gone down that lonely lane with just the laboratory shining white against the Wash. He'd decided to stop her there because, at last, one of these girls was where others wouldn't see him. She'd looked so afraid, so submissive, it had filled his body with strength. But it was more than that, he knew now, she looked guilty.

She thought he'd caught her. Doing what? Living with the knowledge of having killed Geraldine Franson? Perhaps, perhaps not. But she knew something. And he would find out what it was.

Being part of the law was no help now. He didn't need to be a policeman. He could move more freely without their restrictions. He could get her and he could arrange justice.

Re-spray his car. Die his hair. Wear coloured contact lenses. Follow her. It might take a few days. He'd phone in sick. They would forget, at least for a while, about the policeman with no number. With luck Carroll Enderby would have felt too guilty and scared to tell them about him. And they were too busy with the body on the sandbank. It would give him time to get what he wanted before Campbell.

Campbell shut his inner office door. Thursday morning had been devoured by paperwork and people whingeing about incorrectly filled in forms. Such things were nothing to do with him even if the said form requiring the showing of driving documents at the local police station had been given to Carroll Enderby. These things happened every day of the week. And then Flagg had phoned in sick.

All Campbell wanted to do was think. He took out his notebook. He flipped back a page. Ah, the missing evidence from Geraldine's flat. So he called Garden in and asked her to check for any computer data back-up.

'I can't remember taking anything away like that,' she said. 'She could have e-mailed it to some-one, or sent it to a storage site. They're looking at her computer now.'

'Somehow I don't think she would send such sensitive material through the internet, so look anyway, please. And, look at the flat again,' he said thinking he sounded unduly short with her. Ah well, he couldn't always be as polite as he'd like.

He thought he heard her click her tongue like his wife Margaret did when she was cross with him but was not going to be drawn on why. Garden's fuzzy ponytail flicked at him as she left.

Never mind. That's the details thrown up from the last few days dealt with. Now where was he? Ah yes: Lara Elves's story about the body being dumped in the river under the bridge.

Campbell still considered it part of the picture even though everyone else at the police station had discounted it – the lack of anyone to corroborate the story being their reason. Low tide would not usually be the time for dumping in the river, surely? Whatever was being dumped it would get swept back in on the flood tide. So even he had to place Lara's story low on his list of probabilities.

'Now we come to Geraldine,' he said to himself. 'Is Geraldine Franson the body on the sand bank? Forensics are making the body fit her profile more each day. Deep cuts were made before death. How could they have been made? A blade from a tool, a knife? Who would have heard her scream out there with the howling wind? No-one. So who could have cut her and then left her to drown?

He wrote down the names of Brother Joshua Alexander, Brother Michael and Professor Roger Rick despite their alibis. They were not to be forgotten even if Tarnish had made Jenner take them off the display board in the outer office. They may no longer be suspects but they were still part of the picture of Geraldine's life.

Then there was Stranfield and Carroll Enderby from the lab. Though Stranfield had sounded genuine enough when he said he needed Geraldine to continue the work on the computer chip. And, Carroll Enderby was there at every turn Campbell made. She seemed to have entwined herself with Geraldine's disappearance. She had been booked on a course with

106

Geraldine's old tutor – Campbell'd found her fighting with him. Later, Brother Joshua had phoned to say Carroll Enderby had visited him looking for Geraldine. Geraldine's murderer would not behave like this nor would someone who was just a work colleague. These actions were more like a relative or lover who couldn't wait for the police.

He knew so little about Carroll Enderby. He blamed his illness for such neglect. Nor had he taken the opportunity to warn her against involvement in what could well be dangerous situations. He made a note to put this matter right.

There was Geraldine's family to consider also: Mother, Agatha Spier, Uncle, Arthur Franson, and family friend, Jack Wren. He thought of Agatha Spier waiting for her daughter in West Africa. He needed to speak to her, if only through a third party. And Roger Rick had not delivered her to him as he'd hoped. He could wait no longer, he would have to take the flack. He lifted the phone and spoke to Tarnish about Roger Rick's removal of funds from his home country and Agatha Spier's involvement.

Campbell listened to Tarnish yell at him for his oversight in not putting this information into his original report but he would tell the appropriate authorities immediately.

'Phew.' Campbell dropped the phone back in its cradle.

Getting back to his review of the body on Catstail Sandbank he said to himself, 'And lastly there was the man who'd taken Geraldine out on the Wash to collect cockles and mussels every month, Harry Blacking. "The son of a hero," his wife, Renie, had said. But there was something he didn't trust about Renie. It wasn't her dislike of him, it was the way she tried to hide the goings on in the bed and breakfast hotel.

There was still so much to sort out.

'Next, let's suppose the opposite,' said Campbell to himself. 'Let's suppose Geraldine is alive.' He knew such a statement would annoy Tarnish, but alone he could say anything.

'Roger Rick says she's in Africa. To check that I will have to wait for Agatha Spier.'

'There is another possibility: Agatha herself has changed names quite legally twice. It is quite easy for a woman's history to be disguised through marriage. Old Arthur Franson was right about that: it is difficult to know the truth about women. And I think there is a possibility that Geraldine may have voluntarily gone away. If this is the case then it is time for a television appeal.'

He scribbled out a memo to Tarnish, not wishing to disturb him again, and handed it to Jenner in the outer office. He avoided her cool blue eyes telling him he was a coward and turned back to his door.

'Excuse me, Sir,' said DS Jenner, 'I've just had a phone call. Jack Wren is conscious and he's been returned to the local hospital.'

Campbell was again filled with dread. Had he saved this man for a cruel future?

Chapter 11

The hospital always looked to Campbell as if it had landed in blocks and been put together by aliens. But he knew the functional sixties' style of building was identical to many others around the country.

Inside he found Jack Wren's ward and the nursing sister. He could see a man in his seventies with malt-coloured hair looking at an aviation magazine in a utility bed-come-trolley. But before he could approach him he introduced himself to the nursing sister because he had to ask her,

'Is Jack Wren terminally ill.'

'No, I thought you would know that he was overcome by car fumes as you were the one who saved his life,' she replied.

'How did you know that?' Campbell could feel his Edinburgh accent pull strongly across the question with surprise.

'Polly Browme's been in to see him. She told me all about it. She said you hadn't wanted any publicity. She said her husband was furious though it didn't seem to bother Polly much.'

The relief of Jack Wren not suffering from the pains of a terminal illness coursed through his body. Behind this rush he was left weakened, but he made it to Jack Wren's bedside and sat down.

'You look awful,' said the Canadian.

'I hear you're going to live,' said Campbell. He showed his identity card.

'Should I thank you?' asked the patient.

'I don't know,' replied Campbell.

'You want me to tell you why I tried to smoke myself?'

'Aye, please.'

'That'll take a drop of your Scotch Whisky.'

'They only do tea round here.'

'Tea'll have to do.'

Somewhere in a corridor Campbell found a tea machine and hoped the interlude would be enough for Jack Wren to collect himself together for the telling of his story. He pressed the button for tea with milk and extra sugar.

'Would you believe,' said Jack Wren on Campbell's return, 'this is all the result of a sunny beach and a beautiful girl?'

Campbell raised his eyebrows urging him to continue. He settled back to listen to the story explaining that he was still tired himself from illness but he'd found before how, when he was totally exhausted, he was acutely aware of every single word, if he listened with his eyes closed.

Jack Wren started, 'A young woman in a summer dress walking and dancing along the beach – the beach is empty. There is barbed wire along the sand dunes – a British army with guns. They wave and shout at her. All good British summer fun. She waves back and smiles. Then I make out their words. They're telling her to get off the beach. The beach is closed. The beach is mined. But they all stay where they are. No-one goes to her.'

Campbell leaned forward, and Jack continued: '"You must be mad," one soldier says to me as he helps me find a way through. I run. She runs away. I yell at her to stop. I tell her the beach is mined. She stops. I hold her, amazed that I am not already dead, amazed that she is alive.

'We came back in my footsteps.' Jack Wren took a sip of cold tea dregs.

Campbell opened his eyes. 'I'll get you another,' he offered.

'Please. And no sugar this time, if that's OK by you?'

When Campbell returned with the tea Jack Wren continued, 'I was on leave at the time walking on the salt marshes. The affair with Georgina Hawser was brief. And then she wrote and told me she had a child which was mine but she'd married someone else.

'During the war you were told so many lies. Later I guessed that the beach hadn't been mined, just closed off. We were always reminded in those days that eyes were everywhere so these little white lies were acceptable. There were artificial airfields near real ones to mislead the bombers. It was all good tactics.

'I always supported Georgina Brightwood and her daughter Agatha especially when old Brightwood passed away. I came to see them from time to time and when Agatha's daughter, Geraldine, was born I was the happiest man on Earth.

'When Georgina died I was in Canada. I came straight over, but I missed the funeral. Agatha and Geraldine had both booked holidays for afterwards, but Agatha said I could stay on if I wished.

'I'd paid for most of the house anyway. But then the letter came. I had no-one to tell.'

'What letter?' asked Campbell seeing Jack Wren struggling to continue.

'Georgina had arranged to send me a letter after her death. It had been sent to Canada where it had been forwarded back to me here.' Again Jack Wren stopped.

'You don't have to tell me anymore, Mr Wren, if you don't want to.'

'No, no I want to. I need to tell someone.'

Campbell settled back into his seat.

He didn't want to give the impression he was pushing to know this man's private affairs.

'In her letter she told me I should know the truth. She'd already been pregnant when she met me. The child, Agatha, was not mine but Brightwood's all along. I realise now that her attraction that day hadn't been the glow of a young woman inspired by the sea and the sand, but the bloom of early pregnancy. I had been a victim of disinformation. What I can't come to terms with is the fact that she has taken away from me my daughter and my grand-daughter in two sheets of paper.'

'Have you still got the letter?' asked Campbell.

'No, I burnt it before that ridiculous episode in the garage. I'm sorry to have put everyone to so much trouble.'

'You were in shock,' said Campbell.

'I guess I was,' said Jack Wren. He leaned back on his pillows. And Campbell couldn't bring himself to ask him about Geraldine's teeth. To do so would tell him he thought Geraldine might be dead and he didn't think the frail airman inside that once powerful frame could take anymore today.


Curran Elves held the gemstone up to the Friday morning sun rising over the land. He turned to look at the Wash through the green angles of its edges. The air was still. The sky was blue except for strands of clouds forming on the western horizon. They reflected the pinks of the east. Curran thought they looked like people screaming.

And he was screaming inside.

Green gems were unlucky. Everyone knew that. Perhaps it was the cause of his wife's coolness towards him. Lara'd shown no tenderness for his nightmares following his discovery of the body on the sandbank. And she'd slapped him for his drunkenness when he'd tried to drive the memory away with alcohol. You could not trust a green gem in the same way you couldn't trust sunshine and blue skies.

It was as if the gem had been drawn to him in the same way bad luck found him out. Just like the monk standing on the channel wall just before he'd found the body. He'd had no reason to connect the gem with the corpse. So why, he asked himself, had he said nothing to Lara and hidden it when Pet in the pub had spotted it?

He'd feared someone would take it off him. It looked valuable. He was poor. Why not?

He could never take anything from a living human being, let alone a dead one. But that is what people must think. Everyone knew Geraldine Franson's mother was a jeweller. And the police would guess the same way as everybody else. He'd not realised he'd got this evil thing until he'd washed the mussels. It must've been caught in the seaweed they were attached to.

Now he couldn't tell the police. It was too late. They would ask him why he'd said nothing when he'd made his statement. He'd found the body. He would be the simple answer to their problem.

And Harry Blacking knew Curran had it. No doubt Pet had told him. Now he thought about it, the fight between Harry and himself had really changed nothing. His father-in-law could drop the police an anonymous hint any time he liked. And Curran wasn't sure if his threat to tell the police about Harry Blacking would put him off. Because Curran's threat had been empty. He didn't know a thing about his father-in-law's business. He only knew he was as devious as his two-faced so-called hero-father had been before him. And, he could only guess at what Harry did. He hadn't any proof. Police needed proof.

Like a green gem.

He wanted to be rid of Harry and he wanted to be rid of Stranfield who kept finding Curran out each day to ask him what he'd found on the sand banks. He'd told the crab-fleshed man from the laboratory to stay in his square-eyed box of a building and leave the Wash to the fishermen.

As a child Charlotte had told him you could get rid of your troubles by telling them to a stone on the beach and casting them into the sea. Curran looked at the green gem. He'd given it his troubles so now he would return it to the river estuary and, with luck, the cold waters of the North Sea would take it away.

He pulled his arm back and thrust it to the north-eastern horizon where the Wash and the sky joined. His own arm wrenched at his shoulder as the stone shot from his hand. And as Curran watched it arc across the brackish water he swore against being drawn by the sparkle of easy money.

\*               \*               \*

Friday morning Campbell found himself back beside Jack Wren's bedside. He could not put off asking him about Geraldine, Jack's once-upon-a-time grand-daughter, any longer. But he could still hear himself talking about other things.

'If you were stationed in this area during the war you must have met other local people.'

'That's true,' said Jack Wren. 'Most of my buddies came from Canada like myself, but I did get picked out of the sea on one occasion when our Wellington didn't make it back all the way to the airfield. One of the crew came from this area, Bert Blacking. He became quite known for his heroism. I've kept in touch with his family ever since. He has a son, Harry.'

Campbell un-wrapped his willow branch arm from the back of his chair and leaned towards Jack's bed. Harry Blacking not only seemed to know the Wash but everyone who'd come into contact with it. He remembered something Jenner had told him about all people locally being loosely connected to each other. That was sometimes the case even in his home city of Edinburgh so he wasn't going to dismiss the connection between these two men on those grounds.

He really wanted to ask how close Jack Wren had been with Harry Blacking, but to avoid giving away that this might matter he asked, 'Didn't you think about talking to him when you got your letter from Georgina Brightwood.'

'I couldn't.' Jack scraped his forelock of malted white hair back and sighed. 'He knows Geraldine too well. He takes her across the sand banks once a month. He thought she was my granddaughter. I'd made no secret of it since Georgina's husband died.'

The present tense and the solidity of this statement made Campbell look away. 'You could have had a DNA test.' he suggested.

'I suppose I wanted to believe. And, I couldn't see Georgina or Agatha agreeing to it and I wouldn't want to ask Geraldine. What would she think of me?'

'I'm afraid,' said Campbell, summoning up his courage, 'that we've found a body of a woman on Catstail Sandbank. She fits the general description of Geraldine Franson.' Campbell'd hoped that Georgina Brightwood's lies might have hardened Jack Wren against the news, but he'd half-guessed the World War II airman was not the sort of man to be so readily embittered against a girl he'd known for over thirty years as his granddaughter. Campbell laid his hand on Jack Wren's trembling shoulder.

'She's on holiday,' Jack managed to say before laying his ashen face in his long-fingered hands.

The nurse came over. Campbell'd warned her he had bad news and so was not surprised to be bustled away before he could ask any direct questions about Geraldine Franson. And he remembered his fear of giving Jack Wren a future he would not want.

Campbell's paperwork had turned morning into afternoon and Tarnish was wanting everything written down in report form so nothing could be missed out. The tension from the boss's office flowed down the stairs into the outer office surrounding Campbell with echoes from his training. Forgetting to tell Tarnish about Mrs Agatha Spier's smuggling activities was against the rules. And it was clear he'd done it on purpose.

A short coffee break later he found himself in front of Tarnish examining the carefully applied leather trim on his sports jacket's sleeves. This little reminder of Campbell's wife, Margaret, gave him some comfort, though he secretly thought her happiness at whatever strange hours he kept suggested an independence from him that he found slightly unsettling. Still she was a busy artist and you couldn't argue with that.

Campbell centred his gaze on the wall over Tarnish's left shoulder. He was sure Tarnish used his room to intimidate his visitors. The tidiness and unmarked white wall devoid of photographs stared back at him.

'DC Flagg not in,' said Tarnish.

'Off sick,' said Campbell.

'He's a good officer.'

Campbell could see that Tarnish thought Flagg to be like himself in his youth.

'When's Sergeant Parnold coming back?' asked Campbell. Suddenly he missed Parnold on secondment to the Met. Working with him was like wearing an old woollen coat, he thought, scratchy but dependable.

'They've asked him to stay another month and I think we can manage without him here.'

Campbell was about to suggest otherwise – there were so many leads still to follow – when Tarnish said, 'I've decided against your television appeal for Geraldine Franson.'

'Why?' asked Campbell his chest tightening around his windpipe. Tarnish was enjoying himself.

'I've had confirmation from forensics that the hair in Geraldine's hairbrush matches that found on the body from Catstail Sandbank. The body is Geraldine Franson.'

'That would appear to be the case,' said Campbell hoping he sounded as if he was agreeing with his superior officer.

'This Jack Wren person certainly had a motive to kill Geraldine Franson. She and her mother had been taking money off him for years under false pretences. He certainly had a motive.'

'He's old.'

'Geraldine was small. And he's quite tall.'

Friday afternoon had turned Jack Wren from Thursday's sad dispossessed World War II veteran into today's murderer. Campbell felt his face redden but said with Scottish ice in his voice,

'I'm certain Jack Wren had nothing to do with the body on Catstail Sandbank. His grief over the possible death of Geraldine was testament to it.'

'That,' said Tarnish, 'could have been a display of regret from a guilty man. I want you back at that hospital and I want Jack Wren interviewed under caution.'

'He's not well enough. His answers would never stand up in court.'

'I think they will,' said Tarnish. 'This matter is not negotiable, Campbell.'

'I'll have to be guided by the doctors on the timing of such an interview.' Campbell decided to ensure a few days from the medical profession.

'Just make sure you do it.'

'Sir,' said Campbell. It certainly sounded like obedience. He turned and made for the door.

'And, by the way, Inspector Campbell, there's no news about Agatha Spier from Africa yet. The earlier information is passed on the greater the chance of success.'

'Are you alright?' asked Campbell. All he could see through the dimness of the hall outside Tarnish's office and his failing ability to focus through tired eyes was Garden's frizzy brown ponytail bobbing about and flicking, with its owner, from side to side.

'I need to talk to you,' she said. 'I've read your report on your discussion with Arthur Franson.'

Tarnish's harsh rasping voice faded in Campbell's head as he delighted in the result of his determination to spread such information quickly among those involved with the investigation. Tarnish was not, in his opinion required to be on that direct line. He walked away from his boss's door towards the head of the stairs as she continued,

'I've also read your report about Jack Wren. And Tarnish has had the forensic report about Geraldine's hair posted up while you were in his office.'

'Tarnish thinks Jack Wren killed Geraldine,' said Campbell. She might as well know.

'It still might not be Geraldine,' said Garden. 'You don't believe she's dead, do you?'

'Forensics have sucked up the snail trail and told us which snail it is.' Campbell started down the stairs.

'Twins,' said Garden touching his arm. Campbell gently removed her fingers. 'I'm sorry,' she said. 'I meant, supposing Geraldine had a twin - identical. Her father was a twin.'

'I don't think identical twins run in families,' said Campbell. 'My wife's mother was one of twins. It's the un-identical variety that runs in families.' Tarnish had at last taken Geraldine away from him. He'd killed her for Campbell in his mind, slowly over the last hour with his poisoned words. Even this thread of fancy from Garden he could no longer accept.

Why had he wanted her to be alive so much? He'd befriended her empty spaces, her pictures without realising it. After all, there was a dead person to consider and isn't it most likely to be Geraldine?

His arms and legs felt too long for the spacing of the stairs and the height of the banister. Margaret had, of course, been right. He had come back to work too soon after his illness. He really couldn't blame Flagg for taking a couple of days off sick.

Campbell's fever dream came back to him. He'd dismissed the notion of Brother Michael and Brother Joshua being lovers. And he didn't want to remember the part which showed Jack Wren standing over the body in the Wash. He wondered if the connection had always been there in his mind. Dreams weren't proof. He knew that. He hoped this part was as untrue as his view of the monks had been. But then he remembered the baby in Polly Browme's sturdy arms, not her own baby parked close to Jack Wren's rescue but the dream child: the one that carried the face of Lara Elves.

He felt for a moment as if all the young women he'd met in this investigation were identical, like twins:- Lara Elves who helped at the monastery, Carroll Enderby at the laboratory and Geraldine Franson whose face he'd only seen in photographs.

'Our dreams often only express our fears,' he said to Garden.

'I know, Sir. Shall I look into the twins idea?'

'Geraldine's mother is unobtainable that only leaves Jack Wren to speak to and I'm in no hurry to disturb him again.' As the next time I speak to him, he thought, I will probably have to arrest him.

Campbell drew himself together. 'You can check out the birth registrations if you must. But I've made a list of real suspects, Garden. I think we'll continue with that for the time being. And Harry Blacking is the one name that keeps bubbling up to the top. But we've not really got any evidence against him.'

And, he wondered if he could drive from here to home without using his brain because it felt as if someone had dropped an incendiary device in its centre.

Chapter 12

Carroll Enderby stood on top of the sea bank and exposed herself to the chill of the Wash. She'd expected to be blown away but there was just a light wind. The bright blue sky stretched all around her except where it was broken by her squat guide, Harry Blacking. He was level with her but far enough away for her to bear walking out on the mud flats with this stranger. When she'd sat next to him in his land-rover on the way here, she'd found his frequent looks at her unsettling.

Behind her, a field back, at the old sea bank, was the monastery in the World War II look-out tower. She was surprised at how close it was to this spot where Geraldine walked out every month with Harry Blacking.

In front of her, she saw a huge island built up off the sand and mud of the Wash. It was, by its shape, man-made and it reminded her of an ancient burial mound with its crown cut off. It must even stand above the sea at high tide, she thought, because grass as green as that beneath her feet was growing along its top. And, examining the distance, she worked out that it must be even higher than the sea bank. And close to the island a black structure like a watch tower had been built.

Harry Blacking strode down the bank, Carroll followed. Her first foot step on the sand coloured mud covered with grasses thrilled and scared her – like the first taste of alcohol. The vegetation folded under each of her Wellingtons making a raft over the soft mud. She hadn't expected that. When she looked out from the laboratory and saw the sandbanks exposed by the tide, all she'd seen was the sun catching the tops of them making them look like the white sands of a Caribbean beach and there were no reeds or grasses on them. But here, as she glanced up she saw that fifty metres out onto the sand bank they ceased to grow. These grasses, she realised were on the edges of the Wash because the silt was being laid down turning the sea into dry land – the same way the monastery in the old World War II building was now a field in-land standing against the old sea bank.

She heard the broken call of a wader-bird. She couldn't turn to look, she needed all her balance to stay up as the mud sucked at her feet. But the sound had an eerie quality like the echo of a lost scream. It made her think of Geraldine. Harry Blacking had taken her out on the Wash too.

The grass turned to reeds – old, brittle and yellow. The mud became stickier and the reeds grew further apart. From the sea bank this area had looked flat to Carroll, but now she found herself working even harder to cope with the mud, which had been left by the water running out to sea in bumps and dips like huge waves.

Harry Blacking's square back and short legs seemed not to notice the going. He was talking to her over his shoulder, though the sound of it was muted, as was the sound of the wind, by the cotton wool in her ears he'd told her to wear and her woolly hat.

She shouted, 'What did you say?' and he came over to her.

'We've got to cross a creek up here. I'll help you.'

She nodded but she didn't want help. Stranfield must be laughing at her now knowing of her discomfort. She stole a glance at the laboratory but it was too far away to make out clearly.

Geraldine would have had no trouble with getting over the mud – everything always came easily to her. This thought made a great hollow cavity inside Carroll open up. It threatened for a moment to swallow her. She'd tried to cut out of her mind the morning paper's headline of, "Body on Catstail Sandbank named," and below the words "Geraldine Franson", which had jumped out at her. She couldn't cope with the idea that Geraldine might never walk out on the Wash again for the samples of shell fish.

'Do you think,' said Campbell to Jenner, 'that this will work?'

'I spoke to the residential home owner this morning. Charlotte Elves is full of chat since her upset last Saturday. She's from the fishing community, she'll know about all of them. Lara Elves said her father, Harry, probably arranged to upset Charlotte. They have a history, I'm sure of it.'

'And,' said Campbell, 'she'll tell us a lot else besides. I'm not sure if we've the time to be patient with her.' But Jenner had already rung the bell, and a carer soon appeared to take them through.

Sitting in the conservatory, Charlotte looked to Campbell like a frail old vine with her gnarled hands and pale skin. He held out his own long fingers over hers to break her gaze which was fixed there. When he removed his hand she lifted her head and stared directly into his eyes and opened her fingers. Cupped inside them lay the pewter box Jenner had told him about.

'Policeman?' asked Charlotte.

Campbell nodded.

'You can't arrest her now.'

'Who?' asked Campbell.

'Georgina.'

'Georgina who?'

'Georgina Hawser-Brightwood. My sister.'

Campbell looked up at Jenner, she was obviously working out in her head the family tree linking Curran Elves and his clan remotely but definitely to Geraldine Franson – their grandmothers were sisters. He wondered if the rest of their families knew and they had just not bothered to tell him. Harry Blacking had, after-all, not even mentioned he was Curran's father-in-law when they stood together on Catstail Sandbank. Campbell had found it out by accident from Lara.

'I didn't know you had a sister,' said the carer to Charlotte.

'I didn't. From the time she took up with a foreigner I had nothing to do with her. I never even mentioned her name till today.'

So the rest of the families might well not know the connection, thought Campbell. This was just one of those side issues he hadn't got time for, but curiously it had led to someone he was seeking information on, Jack Wren. He took the opportunity to redirect the line of conversation with, 'Was Georgina's man someone from abroad?'

'No, Joseph Brightwood, wasn't from abroad. He wasn't from the fishing end of town. He was a shop-keeper in one of them department stores. Gived her airs and graces, it did – foreign to us fishing folk.'

Campbell looked down to hide his smile. His own mother would have said something similar about her sister a few years ago. Only the words would have been tied together with an Edinburgh knot in her voice instead of Charlotte's broad local ribbon.

'Anyway, she's dead. You're too late. She stole the twin to this box when she married him.'

'Oh dear, I'm sorry,' said the carer.

'I'm not sorry she's dead,' said Charlotte. 'I want the other box back.'

'We,' said Campbell, 'really came to ask about your grandson's father-in-law, Harry Blacking.'

Charlotte spat into the plant pot beside her.

'Charlotte, pet,' said the carer, 'you mustn't do that.'

'Bert Blacking was a hero so they said,' said Charlotte. Campbell noted that she spoke with no apology in her voice. 'Saved airmen during the war, but as soon as the war was over he was up to his old tricks. My husband, Edward, knew what Bert was doing and he soon was drownded in the North Sea. They never found his body.'

'And Bert's son, Harry?' asked Campbell. At last the feeling of vagueness following his illness was slipping away from him.

'There is more blood on his hands than on his father's.' Charlotte paused and looked at the carer. 'This is private,' she said.

'I'll make a cup of tea,' said the carer.


Carroll Enderby peered about the length of a man down into the creek. The mud was thick and grey around her feet and it fell away sharply where the tidal waters had cut the deeper path in front of her. The metre distance between the creek's sides would ordinarily have given her no trouble at all but her boots were already trapped by the gluey mud.

'Lean on me,' ordered Harry Blacking.

She did as she was told, though she didn't like touching him. Her hands gripped the sides of her rubber boots through the folds of her waterproof trousers worn over her footwear. She pulled each boot out of the mud in turn. She thought he was giving her more help than she really needed to stand so she said, 'Thank you.' But his hands started to leave her only slowly making her take a quick step to the side to rid her of them. She pretended she was lightening herself up to jump the creek.

Harry Blacking leapt the creek without any difficulty.

'Quick, before your feet sink in!' he called extending his short arm and stubby fingers towards her.

She didn't want to take his hand so she angled herself away from him. She wanted to jump cleanly. She knew she had a good power to weight ratio, so she ordered herself to: go for it.

Despite the drag from the mud slowing her leap into a sprawl her feet landed together on the other side. Her relief collapsed as the mud held her feet down while her body continued to go forward.

Carroll covered her embarrassment at falling with a laugh but caught a glint of triumph in Harry Blacking's eyes as he helped her back to her feet.

'It gets easier now,' he said.

But her legs were already feeling the distance they'd walked.

Campbell leaned forwards in his chair to listen to the paling tones of Charlotte's voice.

'He killed them all,' she said.

'People in the war?' asked Campbell, purposefully finding difficulties in following her drift. She had to be clearer than this.

'No, of course not,' she snapped back. 'But that's when Bert made the contacts. And he niver lost them.'

'You said, Harry used the Wash for wrong,' Campbell reminded her.

'He's got too bad a taste for the sea or she'd hive taken him long ago. She spat him back once. But he's given her mine: my son and his wife. And he was there with his father when my husband died. He learnt it all from Bert.'

'How did Harry use the Wash for wrong, Mrs Elves,' persisted Campbell using Charlotte's surname to show that he respected her.

'You don't want to know.'

'Aye, I do,' said Campbell.

'He takes things in and out of the country around those sandbanks. Things he shouldn't.'

'And people?' asked Campbell.

'People too,' said Charlotte.

'Thank you,' said Campbell already making plans to find out where Harry Blacking was this morning and arrest him. The chances were he was the one who Geraldine had used to take her in and out of England. As he rose Charlotte said,

'I did know about Jack Wren. That's the foreigner you meant, isn't it, Mr Policeman? He was a tall lean man. Agatha was never his child. She was the image of Joseph Brightwood as a little'un. Always plump, not like us Hawsers at all.'

'I thought you didn't speak to her.'

'Don't stop you looking though.'

'Were you not tempted to tell Jack Wren about the lie.'

'None of my business,' said Charlotte looking at the carer who was approaching with a tray of tea.

'I'm sorry,' said Jenner to the carer, 'We won't be stopping.'

Carroll found Harry Blacking silently insisted on walking next to her now. No matter how slow or fast she tried to adjust her pace, he matched it.

He explained that the markers sticking out of the mud were there to measure the silting of the sand banks and that he guessed the black tower by the island was some sort of watch tower. Then he said, 'You're like the other one.'

'Who?' she managed to ask, despite her concentration on her task of walking.

'Geraldine Franson. I liked her.'

'Oh,' said Carroll.

'Not in that way.' Harry Blacking smiled at her.

Carroll couldn't read it. Was it lust for Geraldine? Lust for her? He looked pleased with himself.

'I used to do jobs for her,' he added.

'What jobs?' asked Carroll stopping.

He looked away like a man who'd said more than he'd intended. 'We've got to keep moving 'cause of the tide,' he said.

For twenty minutes no more was said until Harry Blacking called, 'Here's some.'

'Some what?' asked Carroll her mind was lurching between Harry Blacking and Geraldine and the thought of the body found on Catstail Sandbank. She feared the tick in her voice would break in and give away her fear.

'Cockles,' said Harry Blacking. 'See this dip there's a cockle down here. If you stick your finger in you'll be able to find it and pull it out. If you can see the shell then a wader-bird's got there afore you. If you give us a bag I'll get some over here while you collect them over there.'

Carroll found herself in the shadow of the black watch-tower near the artificial island picking cockles. Her clothing bundled under her waterproofs making her feel bulky in the middle when she bent down to the mud. But she found a peculiar satisfaction in the exercise and her fears subsided.

'Blasted things.' Flagg blinked over his new brown-coloured contact lenses and tried to focus the binoculars. That man at the laboratory, Stranfield, had told him straight away where Carroll Enderby was. Pretending to be a policeman one more time had been easy. And Stranfield had sounded pleased.

"Stay calm," he told himself. Cool down. Hunt now. Taste the air: salt and marsh, wet grass. Look again, on the horizon: a boat beached on a sandbank. Lower binoculars: an island. Lower again: black tower, two people. Carroll Enderby and her guide, that's what Stranfield had told him.

All he had to do was wait and he would have her. He would have her knowledge. He scraped his hands through his black died hair. He liked the strange hardness the colour gave his white skin.


Carroll Enderby looked at her plastic bag of cockles. At least she had done half the job Stranfield had sent her out to do. Soon she'd be back on dry land. She would have to suffer a lift back to her own car parked back in town, but then she would be free of Harry Blacking.

She was grateful that her rubber gloves kept out the cold and damp from her hands. There were only the mussels to get now. She asked Harry Blacking about them.

'They're easy,' he said.

His leer she read as a threat as he tipped his bag of creamy shelled cockles into hers.

'The mussels attach themselves to sea-weed,' he continued. 'They're on the surface. Look, there's some. Some places they grow them on ropes. They're natural grown here.' When they got to the location he'd pointed out, he said, 'The body on Catstail Sandbank looked like a crop of these from a distance.'

Carroll's nerves in the back of her neck pulsed, bristling the fine hairs along her spine. 'I don't really want to know,' she said managing to control the tick in her voice. And she saw he was filled with triumph. She wanted to run but she stayed to complete her agreement with Stranfield. She wouldn't be put off by this nasty man. Her job depended on it. Just a few more minutes and they would be on their way back to the mainland. She needed Harry Blacking to guide her back. The shifting sands could disappear into sea or quick sand – Geraldine had told her once. After they reached firm ground she would not be taking a lift from him back to her car. She took out her mobile phone to call for a taxi.

'There's no signal out here for an ordinary mobile phone,' said Harry.

She looked at it. He was right. She put it away. She would have to call in at the monastery and try to avoid Renie Blacking. Brother Joshua would phone a taxi for her.

As Carroll bent down to the black shiny shells Harry Blacking whispered in her ear, 'I can do things for you.'

'No, thank you,' she said filling her bag with one scoop of her hand.
'Geraldine Franson was grateful.'

'Was she?' Carroll's voice cracked on the last word. She got up, stuffed
her bags of shell fish into the large pockets of her waterproof and started to
run for the sea bank. She hoped he would follow so she could be sure of
the way but keep far enough from him so he couldn't touch her. Fear
dragged her boots out of the mud and numbed the ache in her legs. Then
she found their outward going footprints. She could go faster now.

At the creak she stopped. She glanced at the trickle of water in the
bottom. When she looked around she could see Harry Blacking was well
back and she could just hear him shout, 'Wait.'

Looking up at the sea bank she was close enough to see a man standing
there. Was he watching her? No, surely not, she told herself. She knew she
must prevent her imagination running away with her. It had to be just a
bird-watcher. But there was something familiar about his stance.

Campbell left his car in the monastery car park and noted Harry
Blacking's was also there. Harry Blacking was taking Carroll Enderby out on
the Wash as per Stranfield's instructions; Renie Blacking had said so. And
Renie was well away from here, still standing in for the owner down at the
bed and breakfast. Jenner had been instructed not to give her any hint that
they were arranging to pick Harry Blacking up for questioning when she
asked Renie where her husband was. She was good at that.

Harry Blacking must have picked Carroll Enderby up from somewhere
as her car was not here or, perhaps, she'd already left, decided Campbell.

Two other police cars pulled up after Campbell, but he didn't want to
wait for them. He was sure now that Harry Blacking was connected in some
way to Geraldine Franson and he was going to find out how. In the corner
of the monastery yard there was a large play pen retaining a pair of toddlers.
He smiled: Lara Elves's bairns. Despite her parents there was something
charming about this local girl's very natural love of family.

But he would still have to get Harry Blacking into one of these police
cars without Lara Elves getting too upset, but, he decided, she might be
easier to handle than her mother.

He took the footpath between the old sea bank and the newer one. He
noted, with approval, the wooden decking that had been provided for the
benefit of easy access to the sea bank. Jenner, Garden and the other
occupants of the police cars followed him. The lush grass was growing

through the boards and gave his shoes little grip but he was happy to walk briskly. This was the only way back from the sea bank for some distance. Harry Blacking would have to come this way to his car.

Ordering the others to stay out of sight, Campbell scanned the Wash from the sea bank and saw Harry Blacking walking over the marsh grasses towards him. At the bank Harry looked up at Campbell. The guide's face was reddened and his eyes were smarting.

'Where's Carroll Enderby?' asked Campbell.

'Haven't you seen her? She came this way. '

'We've only just arrived.'

'She ran away.'

'On the Wash?'

'Back to the mainland.'

'I've not seen her,' said Campbell.

'She ran this way,' insisted Harry Blacking, stumbling.

Campbell knew he still only had enough strength to keep himself up so he beckoned for help and two policemen came and supported Harry Blacking on either side.

'I hint done nothing to her,' said Harry Blacking.

Campbell watched the guide's angular face crumple and then cry. It seemed totally out of character. He nodded to Jenner who carried out the formal arrest.

Campbell, with Garden's help, held Lara's small frame back trying to avoid her pregnancy as the police officers placed her father in one of the cars. He could see Brother Joshua comforting a small child in each arm by the kitchen door and Brother Michael next to him in his wheelchair glaring at the police cars.

'He's done nothing wrong,' Lara screamed at Campbell.

'Have you seen Carroll Enderby today?' he asked Lara, letting her go. And just in case she didn't know the person by name he added, 'She's a small dark haired woman in her mid-twenties.'

Lara glared at him. 'I saw her go out on the Wash with my dad earlier. But I think you know that.' She watched her father sitting in the police car.

'And what about you, Brothers?' asked Campbell.

'We've been in prayer all morning, Inspector,' said Brother Joshua, 'until your noise disturbed us.'

'Is there any chance Carroll could be hiding here?' asked Campbell.

'No,' said Brother Joshua. 'All the doors open on to this courtyard and they've all been locked except the kitchen where Lara was working.'

Lara's jaw was set in a stubborn pout.

'A full picture of what happened this morning might help your father,' Campbell offered.

Lara frowned, her chin softened. 'Though I did see another car come up here about half an hour ago. Carroll Enderby could've gone away in that one.'

'Are you sure you saw another car?'

'Course I am. I don't tell lies.'

But no-one ever saw the same things she did, thought Campbell, so he asked her, 'What was it like?'

'Big black car, pulled up in the lane, didn't park in our car park like most do.'

'Did you write down the number?'

'Course I didn't, I hint got time for that. I saw the driver though. Black hair and white skin.'

'Did you see the car go?'

'No, I just come out here to check on the kids and it was gone.'

Campbell looked at Brother Joshua. He just shrugged negatively back at him. His prayers struck Campbell as being a difficult excuse to argue against. And it was clear that Carroll Enderby wasn't going to be easily found. He nodded to the police car with Harry Blacking in it. The engine started and Lara Elves screamed again,

'He's done nothing wrong.'

'You know it doesn't look good for your father,' said Campbell. And, when she'd screamed herself out, he explained, 'Two women have walked out on the Wash with your father, Geraldine Franson and, this morning, Carroll Enderby. These same two women have disappeared.'

Lara crumpled.

'We'll look after Lara now,' said Brother Michael.

'And we'll pray for Carroll Enderby's safe return,' said Brother Joshua.

Campbell felt dismissed and found himself only partially grateful. He knew he had to interview Harry Blacking but to be so readily excluded from the monks' lives felt like a seam being rapidly sewn to repair a gaping hole so he couldn't see inside it. He spoke to one of his officers and turned to the monks.

'I've already arranged,' he said, 'for the Coastguard to start searching for Carroll Enderby and I've got some officers coming down to cover the sea bank area. I would be grateful if you'd stay away. They'll be extremely busy.' Even if they'd offered to help look for Carroll Enderby, he would have declined. He just didn't want them weaving themselves any further into this tapestry of an investigation.

Chapter 13

Campbell pushed the daily paper on the floor. Tarnish had been so quick to tell the press. Campbell didn't want to be told again that Geraldine was dead.

He fast forwarded the recording over the legal niceties of the interview to the point which he wanted to hear again. Harry Blacking hadn't wanted, 'no lawyer', though he had phoned his wife. Campbell knew Tarnish wanted him to interview Jack Wren and that he would tear around his office like a crazed animal when he found out, but he was safe for now. Saturday afternoon Tarnish would be on the golf course. So with closed eyes Campbell listened to the changing voices.

Jenner: You said you picked up Carroll Enderby and brought her down on the mud flats. We've found her car at the car park on the edge of town like you said, and Lara told us that she saw you both go out along the path by the monastery. So what happened out there today?

Harry Blacking: Nothing. We got out there collecting the shell-fish and she just up and ran away.

Jenner: She wouldn't do that without a reason.

Harry Blacking: She might've been scared of the tides. How should I know?

Jenner: Did you say anything to frighten her?

Harry Blacking: No.

Jenner: Did you talk to her about the body on Catstsail Sandbank?

Harry Blacking: No.

There was a pause.

Campbell: When was the last time you took Geraldine Franson out on the Wash?

Harry Blacking: Four weeks ago. Because of the tides it works out that way.

Campbell: We know she came back safely from that trip because she went into work until she left for her holiday two weeks later. Did you see her again in that time?

Harry Blacking: No.

Campbell: I understand you take other things across the Wash. A little smuggling.

Campbell remembered the tiny shift in Harry Blacking's eyes before they levelled back at him, and he answered, 'Never.'

Campbell: Your father and Geraldine's father were old war time buddies?

Harry Blacking: What's that got to do with it?

Campbell: Wouldn't it be logical for Geraldine to use a friend to get her in and out of the country? A friend she could trust?

Harry Blacking: I hint done nothing wrong. I hint killed nobody.

Campbell: I'm not saying you have. I just want to know if you, at any time, helped Geraldine Franson leave or enter the country.

Harry Blacking: No.

There was another, longer, pause.

Jenner: Did you kill Carroll Enderby?

Harry Blacking: No.

Jenner: Did you kill Geraldine Franson?

Harry Blacking: No.

Campbell turned off the machine. Neither he nor Jenner had got anything out of him after that.

'I need,' he told his map on the wall, 'a way of prizing that man's mouth open. And I think I know how.'

He went into the outer office and called for Jenner.


Jenner found herself peering into the dusty interior of the Bed and Breakfast establishment with Renie Blacking clucking behind her,

'You've got my husband, what more do you want?' and then, 'This is so unsettling for my guests.'

She was surprised at how calm Renie Blacking was. After all, earlier Jenner had skimmed over the reasons for wanting to know where her husband was when they'd wanted to question him. She gathered that Renie Blacking must be hard.

But Jenner couldn't read Campbell's face. He hadn't told her much either so she knew he was just guessing that there was something wrong here. No search or arrest warrants had been applied for, but she knew he would be careful.

'I've come to see,' said Campbell, 'Arthur Franson.'

'I don't know what you want with him.' said Renie Blacking. 'He's an alcoholic. You won't get no sense out of him.'

Jenner glanced from her feet on the bare staircase to Campbell's long legs in front of her and back again as they went up to Arthur Franson's room.

When they entered the alcoholic looked to her as if he'd just had enough drink to flatten the worst of his morning shakes but not enough to endanger his reason. He perched back on his bed and Campbell stood halfway between the bed and the door. Jenner tried to hold her gut against the smell of urine in the hall and that of stale old man in Arthur Franson's room.

'I've looked up your record,' said Campbell. Jenner knew his amiable Edinburgh tones were natural but also useful.

'I am the victim,' said Arthur Franson, 'of an uncaring society.' He patted his thin grey pillow.

'All petty stuff,' agreed Campbell, 'just breaking and entering cars and houses. You wanted somewhere cosy to sleep.'

'It's a man's right.'

'But you're not as comfy here as you thought you might be?'

Jenner sat down on the only chair in the room after checking it. Campbell looked as if he was going to take longer than usual to extract Arthur Franson's information.

'It's all very comfortable,' said Arthur Franson, waving his arm to embrace the room.

'But you're safe,' said Campbell with a slight snip in his tone.

Arthur Franson stood up from his bed. This remark had been calculated to get a reaction, Jenner was sure. And she rose too to match any challenge Arthur Franson might think about making.

'I don't know what you mean,' said Arthur Franson. But Jenner could see fear darting across his blood shot eyes. There was nothing in this alcoholic that was dangerous as far as she could see. He was standing because he was ready to run away.

'Has anyone ever died here?' asked Campbell.

'Never.'

'No tired old wino popping his clogs or over-dosed junkie? No-one tipped themselves off the scales because of money problems?'

Arthur Franson's eyes grew wide startled by Campbell's sharp questioning. 'Not that I know of. People get better. I've seen it all the time.'

'Will you get better?'

'No, I'm safe. '

Jenner watched Campbell catch the words fallen from Arthur Franson before the alcoholic had realised they were gone. 'Safe, but you won't get better?'

Campbell rocked back on his heels and up onto the balls of his feet. He was totally in control, and Arthur Franson was ready to give himself over to that control.

'I'm safe because of my criminal record,' said Arthur Franson. 'There are pictures of me, finger prints.'

'So what about the people who get better?' asked Jenner unable to hold herself back any longer.

'They are renewed. Replaced with fit healthy people. They take their identities and leave.' Arthur Franson lifted his pillow, pulled out his bottle and sat back down on the bed. 'I shall be punished.'

'No, you won't,' said Campbell. 'What happens to ...' He paused. 'The bodies of the unfit.'

'There's been a lot of digging in the yard.'

'Thank you, Mr Franson. We'll make sure you're safe. Come down stairs with us.'

Jenner opened the door while Campbell helped Arthur Franson with his shoes and steered him out of the room.

Jenner, having spent several minutes on the radio in her car delivering Campbell's instructions, saw her boss take the front steps at the B & B in two strides. She locked the car.

Arthur Franson bleated, 'Don't leave me.,' at her, but she followed Campbell anyway.

Renie Blacking was pushing grips into the side of a head scarf to attach it to her bottle-chestnut curls.

'About to clean out a room?' asked Campbell of Renie as Jenner reached him.

'As a matter of fact, yes. One of our people came into some money so they've left. He said he would be forever grateful.'

'Is it the same room you were collecting the laundry from when I called last?'

'What has that old alcy been telling you?' asked Renie Blacking. 'You can't believe a word he tells you. Anyway, what've you got him in your car for?'

'For our enquiries regarding the body on Catstail Sandbank.'

'He int strong enough to kill nobody.'

'Going back to your November spring cleaning, Mrs Blacking, I wondered where the former occupant of that room has gone.'

'He didn't leave a forwarding address.'

'I see.' Campbell got out his note book.

'He's not dead,' said Renie Blacking.

'Why should I think he might be dead, Mrs Blacking?'

'Because of what Arthur told you.'

'I wouldn't disclose what Arthur Franson has told me to you or to anyone else.'

Jenner could see Renie Blacking wrapping her bright red cardigan about her as if she'd caught a sudden chill.

'I believe your husband has a little trade, smuggling. Does he bring in people, Mrs Blacking – foreigners you can accommodate here at the B & B? And better than that, you can give them identities, genuine identities, identities belonging to people who've lived here.'

Renie Blacking stared at him. Jenner thought it was a witch's stare, trying to lay a curse on him.

'You'll have to ask the owner when he comes back. I don't know nothing about it.'

'Laundry, room cleaning? The owner was away when I called last,' said Campbell. 'And what, might I ask, did you do with the people who lived here?'

'We don't kill them, if that's what you mean. They all died natural. My Harry will tell you. '

'What does your husband know of all this?' asked Jenner. She knew she'd sealed the flow of escaping information when Renie Blacking looked at her.

'You'll have to ask him. I int saying a word more.'

And Jenner knew Campbell would not reproach her for putting in the direct question, because all he'd say was, 'Direct questions have to be asked.'

'Your wife,' said Campbell to Harry Blacking in the interview room, 'is being questioned by immigration officers and then she will be interviewed by us. We have officers digging up the yard at the B & B in relation to the whereabouts of some of its ex-residents.'

'I had nothing to do with it,' said Harry Blacking.

'That's not what your wife says. "Ask Harry," she said.'

Campbell glanced at Jenner. 'I heard her myself,' she confirmed for him.

'I hint killed nobody,' said Harry.

'Tell us what you know Harry. You know that's the only way to clear yourself of what's been going on at that place.'

Campbell watched Harry bow his head. He'd played a hunch at the B & B: a combination of Renie's secretiveness and Charlotte's story of the Blacking's trade. But the whole business had turned out to be far deeper and darker than a few illegal immigrants. He'd almost been able to smell the fear of death coming off Arthur Franson when he'd said the word 'safe'. Campbell had only meant that Arthur Franson was now safe from arrest as he didn't have to break in anywhere to sleep.

'People want to live in this country,' said Harry Blacking. 'I don't for the life of me know why.'

'And so you arrange it for them.'

'Yes. And that's all.'

'We'll need all the names involved, Harry,' said Jenner.

'I'll give them to you. But you must know I hint killed nobody.'

Campbell leaned back in his chair and rubbed a hand across his aching neck. He was beginning to need his bed. 'I think,' he said, 'you must tell us about Geraldine Franson.'

'That don't seem so important now,' agreed Harry Blacking. 'Her work was just a bit extra. In and out of the country just when she liked. It was easy.'

'And what about the last time she left the country at the end of October?' asked Campbell.

'I didn't take her out, and that's the truth. She told me she was going on holiday and I believed her. Why shouldn't I? I wished her a good trip and that was that.'

Campbell's mind reeled back as if it had been punched. He was so sure Harry Blacking had taken Geraldine Franson out of the country.

'Did she make any arrangement for you to take her out of the country that she didn't keep?' asked Campbell.

'No. '

'What about cancelling an arrangement? Did she do that?'

'No. I tell you, no.'

'And Carroll Enderby?' asked Campbell.

'She ran away.'

'Why?' asked Jenner.

'I scared her like you said. It was just a bit of fun.'

'And now,' said Campbell, 'she's missing too. It's just as well she's not a resident of the B & B or we might find her replaced in the morning with a healthy person whose English isn't so good.' For a moment Campbell felt the loss of Carroll Enderby like a cut in his side. It matched the cut made in his other side by Tarnish insisting Geraldine Franson was dead. Only sleep would dress the wounds and then he would be able to hunt down the cure.

Harry Blacking wasn't going anywhere and Campbell knew none of them could proceed without sleep. Even the searchers for Carroll Enderby would wait until light before restarting their search. And he would be happy to leave the mess at the B & B for others to tidy up.

Now, perhaps, Tarnish would have to send for Parnold from his secondment at the Met. In addition, he would have to get other police from neighbouring forces. He made the call and the thought of his senior officer suffering some discomfort on a Saturday night gave him some pleasure as he made his way home.

Carroll Enderby leaned against the monastery wall and looked up at the stars. She'd thought she was going to die out on the mud flats. She wasn't sure which bit of her freezing body hurt the most, her starved intestines or her trembling legs. She hadn't dared to eat the un-cleansed, uncooked shell-fish in her pockets. And when she'd scattered them in the mud because she could no longer manage any extra burden and keep walking she'd said goodbye to her job. Money would have to wait. And something in her depths, which Brother Joshua would no doubt call her soul, told her that the tall strong monk would look after her.

Glancing around the only light she could see was in the office so she tapped on the window. A few moments later Brother Michael's local accent came through the glass.

'Who's there?'

'I need to see Brother Joshua.' Carroll hadn't wanted another run in with Brother Michael, but her body was screaming for rest.

'He's asleep, Carroll,' said Brother Michael. He sounded irritable. Then he paused before saying in kinder tones, 'But I'll let you in. Wait a minute.'

Having shown Carroll into the sitting room she'd been in before with the blue flowered chairs, Brother Michael in his wheelchair buzzed away to get her some dry clothes, towel, and blankets. His friendliness unsettled her. Among the things he returned with were: a man's vest, shirt and jeans. They were too small to have ever belonged to Brother Joshua. For a moment she didn't want to wear Brother Michael's old clothes.

'Brother Joshua,' he said, 'has spoken to me about my attitude towards you and I have prayed for the strength to change myself. I'll leave you for a while and make you some hot chocolate and porridge.' He paused. 'I've left some string as well so you can parcel up your damp clothes in the newspaper.' His wheelchair bumped the door jamb as he manoeuvred it out of the room.

Carroll, feeling too weak to question his charity, took off her filthy clothes on the sheets of newspaper and put on the replacements. She folded the remnants of her day's survival on the mud flat together and parcelled it up with the string as directed. She didn't want the monks to be burdened by her mess.

As she supped her hot chocolate and porridge Brother Michael parked his wheelchair opposite her and said, 'I have to warn you the police are after you. '

Carroll put down her bowl next to her cup.

'There was one on the sea bank while you were out on the mud flats with Harry Blacking. I told him it wasn't you out there, but bait diggers. The policeman said that it was you and that he had information to that effect. I said Harry Blacking had told me the trip was cancelled.'

'Why did you say that?'

'I don't know. I just didn't like the look of him. '

'So why didn't he wait anyway?'

'I told him he was blocking the lane. He didn't seem interested in coming into the car park.'

'What did he look like?'

'Black hair, white skin. Odd looking man. But he showed me his identification.'

'Did he say why he was looking for me?' She could feel her throat tightening. It didn't sound like DC Flagg or the Scottish Inspector. But it didn't surprise her. She'd gone across to Newington University only to entangle herself with Roger Rick. She'd run across the mud flats to escape Harry Blacking. She'd gone back out there because of that man standing on the new sea bank. She'd failed to convince herself that he was a bird watcher. She was no surprised to find he was a policeman. There were people after her everywhere. She knew she was cornered by her own dishonesty.

'The policeman didn't say what he wanted, but don't worry,' said Brother Michael. 'I've got a place you can stay for a while, until they sort out this business.'

Carroll knew she couldn't cope with police questioning. Her guilt at stealing information about the laboratory would soon come out, and she was sure that would mean a prison sentence. And she'd done nothing to Geraldine Franson so, if left long enough, the police would find Geraldine's murderer and even they would leave her alone.

She followed Michael along a corridor that ran behind the sitting room she'd just been in and towards the corner where the look-out tower reached up towards the night sky. A metre in front of what Carroll thought must be the entrance to the tower Brother Michael stopped and pointed down at a rectangle formed in the parquet flooring.

'We tell people it's a drainage manhole cover, but it's an old bomb shelter. Pull the ring. It should come up easily enough.'

She did as she was told and found herself looking down an old concrete stairway which soon disappeared into darkness.

'I'll need a light,' she said.

'There's a camping light in the kitchen. Come with me.'

As he directed her to the top of the kitchen cabinet he asked in a hushed voice, 'Why did you run away from Harry Blacking?'

'I thought he was going to kill me.' Carroll spoke quietly too so as not, she assumed, to wake Brother Joshua. She picked up the battery powered lamp.

'Why did you think he might kill you?'

'Because of the things he said and the way he said them.'

'There are spare batteries up there too,' said Brother Michael. 'So how did you hide from Harry Blacking out there?'

'I got in the creek and worked my way along it until I got to a bend. Then I carried on further until I thought I was far enough away not to be seen clearly. Doubling back across the mud flat to the island I didn't think I was going to make it before the tide came in so I took refuge in the old black watchtower out there. It creaked. I thought it might break.' Carroll went down into the bomb shelter with the light and batteries. She put down her load and returned to the hatch.

'You chose well. A helicopter would have seen you on the island. And they were looking for you. '

'I did see a helicopter go by, but I'd already decided to risk coming back in the dark.'

'You were lucky to get back here at all at night.'

'I know.'

Leaning on the bomb shelter steps Carroll looked at Brother Michael. 'I'm sorry about all that nonsense about the money before.'

'And I am sorry too,' said Brother Michael passing her some blankets he'd carried across his knees. 'There's a bed and a toilet down there. And I'll bring you food regularly. You can stay there as long as you want.'

Carroll felt the thud of the hatch slam shut behind her. It startled her despite reasoning that Brother Michael would not have been able to close it any other way. She wondered if its noise had woken Brother Joshua.


Campbell's Sunday breakfast was interrupted by Margaret shouting, 'Sally Garden's here: says she's found out about that photograph. And what was that you were muttering about this morning? Something about my mother, wasn't it?'

'She was a twin,' said Campbell finding his wife in her workroom which overlooked the front garden. She was pinning a ribbon to one of her fabric sculptures.

'Yes, my aunt and her were identical twins,' she said.

'When her sister came to the funeral it was as if the ghost of your mother was there.'

'You are fanciful, Raymond. They were so different in many ways. They were two separate people. '

'But with the same genes.'

'Don't keep Sally waiting, Raymond,' said Margaret peering over the support she used for her sculptures. And then she winked at him and looked back at her work.

Garden took him to the top end of his own village, close to the Norman tower of the parish church.

'Polly Browne,' she said, 'was the photographer who took the picture of the Franson brothers and Geraldine at that commemorative service you wanted to know about.' Garden led the way to a cottage behind the church and knocked on the door. Campbell stood back so didn't see who opened the door as he followed Garden in.

He found that the Browme's hall walls were covered with the pictures which were clearly Polly's pleasure as well as her profession. And there was Polly Browme just as he remembered her from the day she'd called him to Jack Wren's attempted suicide. But now her rounded body and face were inviting, instead of set in panic. She led them through to the dining room putting a finger to her lips to indicate that they must be quiet. Once seated at the round teak table that nearly filled the small room, except for a battered roll top bureau at the far end, she said,

'Derek's still asleep and the baby's just gone down.'

Campbell frowned. Just the mention of that man's name made him wince.

Garden reeled off a number she'd, no doubt, been given by the newspaper office as a reference.

'That was five years ago,' said Polly Browme, 'long before Derek came to work at the paper.'

Campbell found a discomfort in his throat which could only be cleared with a cough.

'He's not always like that,' said Polly shuffling through the contents of a folder. 'He told me about looking around your bedroom when you were ill. I was furious. But he feels the responsibility of our daughter rather heavily. He thinks he ought to be in big time journalism and, I'm afraid, it's made him rather unpleasant. And it's all so unnecessary. I shall be going back to work when Clara's six months old.' She passed him a picture.

Yes, this was the one of the twins, Herbert and Arthur Franson, with Herbert's daughter Geraldine that had been in Geraldine's flat. Campbell noted that Tarnish hadn't given this picture to the press when he'd told them about Geraldine Franson being the body on Catstail sandbank; he'd used her identity photo from the laboratory instead.

'Did you,' Campbell asked, 'know Herbert and Arthur Franson?'

'No, I didn't. I didn't even realise it was them until now. So this is Geraldine? Derek will be pleased. I'm a freelance, you see. I own the rights to this photo. I should be able to sell it to the nationals. Derek's always saying I should make up a file of the captions on the computer so I can search for names in the news. But I never got around to it.'

Campbell heard a baby cry upstairs and Polly pushed past them, smiling and nodding, to go and see to her. Left with Garden his gaze strayed from the photo to the desk. He rose from his chair and tried the roll top lid. It was unlocked.

'Sir?' said Garden.

Her one word told him what he knew already: he shouldn't be doing this. He didn't usually look without consent or warrant.

'There is a natural justice in this, Garden,' he said. 'You saw him in my bedroom. Now I think it's my turn to see what he has hidden.' As he said this he watched the lid slide up, and saw a file lying on the writing table part of the bureau. It was marked with the name of Stranfield's laboratory so he opened it.

'What's going on?' came Polly's voice from behind him.

He turned round to see her in the doorway with her baby over her right shoulder. 'Your husband has a file on the place where Geraldine Franson and Carroll Enderby worked,' he said.

'That's not really surprising, is it? He's a newspaper man. Geraldine Franson has been found dead and I heard on the radio this morning that Carroll Enderby has disappeared.'

'He's dated some of these papers. Some are from before Geraldine Franson went missing.'

Campbell saw Derek Browme wiping his gold rimmed spectacles as he came up behind Polly and their baby.

'You didn't tell me they were coming,' he accused his wife.

'I think, Derek, you've got some explaining to do,' said Polly. 'I'll put Clara in her bouncy seat and make us all a cup of tea.'

Campbell listened while Garden took notes about Derek Browme's investigations into the laboratory until Polly returned.

'Have you told them about Carroll Enderby?' she asked.

Derek shook his head. Campbell thought he recognised regret in the journalist's movements.

'He asked her to look for information against her employers,' said Polly. 'He was sure they were up to something illegal. But she found nothing.'

'I told her we could make a lot of money through the nationals.'

'Oh Derek, you didn't.'

'I did.' Derek looked up at his wife and down again before taking off his glasses and wiping his eyes. 'The only information she gave me was a list of investors. And I could have got that readily enough from other sources.'

'I will have to take these papers,' said Campbell.

'Yes, of course,' said Derek Browme. A wave of softness washed over Derek. He went over and picked Clara out of her bouncy seat.

Campbell squeezed around the table to get to the hall.

'Aren't you going to arrest me?' asked Derek Browme as Campbell passed him.

Campbell gave a Celtic sigh and said, 'I really have more important things on my mind at the moment.' Taking the papers he strode from the cottage. Behind him he could hear Garden making their 'goodbyes' for him. And he hoped she would not say any more to him about twins during their journey back to the police station.

Jenner stood inside Flagg's open garage door. She was annoyed with Tarnish. He'd phoned her this morning and told her he wanted her to check on Detective Constable Flagg's illness. It was Sunday for heaven's sake!

She called, 'Flagg,' several times as she picked her way through sprays of dark blue paint, newspaper and rucks of used masking tape. The stink of paint thinners caught in her nose as she knocked on the inner door. He couldn't be out. He wouldn't leave the garage open like this with all his tools out, just asking to be pinched. She called his name again. Perhaps he'd collapsed or had an accident. She guessed he lived on his own. She turned the door handle and pushed.

Dusty brown cord carpet stairs rose in front of her. She hadn't expected Flagg's place to be like this with his immaculate dress and tidy desk in the office. At the top she stepped into his studio style living room and stopped. She called Flagg's name again because she feared from the destruction in front of her that Flagg had been attacked. Sliding around the edge of the room to avoid disturbing anything she checked the other rooms for Flagg, but she did not find him. So she went out the way she'd come and radioed Campbell.

Chapter 14

Campbell looked at the evidence before him. His fingers felt corseted inside his nitrile gloves. The finger print experts were due to arrive soon, so Jenner had said.

Jenner's collection from the garage included the remains of a bright orange decal similar to that found on the livery of police vehicles and two sets of letters that could make the word 'POLICE' twice.

Garden's exhibits included memory sticks for the computer, and a stained tube of black hair die. Garden told him, on being asked, that she'd never found any back-up records for Geraldine's computer he'd asked her to look for in the evidence room. Now Campbell knew where they had gone.

There was a shadow in Campbell's head about an incorrectly filled in form requiring the presentation of driving documents by Carroll Enderby, now a missing person. So he sent Garden back into Flagg's house to find a sample of his writing in its natural, scruffiest form. Within moments she returned with a piece of paper, which she handed to him.

Who was the person who'd given Carroll Enderby that form? And who had wrecked Flagg's home?

He couldn't answer his first question yet, and he wasn't sure if its answer wasn't the same as the answer to his second question.. Campbell had found nothing other than damage in Flagg's home despite Jenner's shocked voice when she'd contacted him: no Flagg dead or alive.

Where was the car that had been converted from police livery? And where was Flagg?

Campbell had ways of looking into the problem of the altered car. He would get Jenner to contact each of the force's stations and check if any of their vehicles were missing and he would set Garden to finding out the index number of Flagg's own car. There were no number plates slung down with the other debris so whichever car it was that had been changed it was still possible that it would have its own number.

Campbell wasn't sure what he was up against. The likelihood was that someone had done this to Flagg, but he couldn't rule out that the police officer himself might have wrecked the place. This latter possibility could make Flagg the unbalanced man stopping people in a pretend police car. Could that really be Detective Constable Flagg? He was arrogant, but was he capable of intimidating people for the sake of it? And what about stopping Carroll Enderby? The form requesting her to show her documents had been dated, and the time marked on it showed that she'd been stopped prior even to Campbell's visit to the attempted suicide of Jack Wren, let alone the discovery of the body on the sandbank. So, if Flagg had been the one driving around in a police livery car, Carroll Enderby being stopped would have just been a strange coincidence.

Unwanted, another possibility popped into Campbell's head: whoever stopped Carroll Enderby could have killed the body on Catstail Sandbank. He still couldn't bring himself to call it Geraldine Franson. The two women did, after all, work at the same laboratory. But for what reason could Flagg have wanted to kill them? Could he have a connection to the laboratory?

Jenner pushed a paper into Campbell's hand. 'I brought it with me this morning.'

Campbell opened his fingers and saw the ticket that Sergeant Porter had made such a fuss about. He compared the hand writing with that on the piece of paper Garden had found for him. They looked the same. 'You thought Flagg might have something to do with this?' asked Campbell.

'Yes, I spoke to Sergeant Porter. He said Flagg behaved really oddly when Carroll Enderby brought it in. And then Flagg went off sick,' said Jenner.

'So you think the car done out in police livery was his?' asked Campbell.

'Yes, I do,' replied Jenner.

'We still have to check the possibility that a police car has been stolen and stripped,' said Campbell. Sadness formed a lump in his chest. Flagg was no longer a colleague. 'Do you know if Flagg had any connection with the laboratory? Could he have had a reason to harm or attack Geraldine Franson and Carroll Enderby?'

'I don't know of any,' said Jenner flatly.

'Plenty of people seem to have suspected the laboratory of pollution,' suggested Campbell.

'He's never struck me as an eco-warrior,' said Garden.

'And it doesn't check out. All the environmental reports are clear. There are no signs of pollution to the Wash from the laboratory,' said Jenner. 'Flagg would have known that.'

He sent Jenner and Garden to do the tasks he'd decided upon regarding the cars and told them to give central communications Flagg's registration number and the number of any missing police cars. They had more chance of finding him through this simple piece of information than anything else, whether someone had taken Flagg or not.

Garden dallied until Campbell asked, 'Yes?'

'Could Flagg have Carroll Enderby?' asked Garden with an edge of concern in her voice.

'I don't know. We'll find out when we find him,' said Campbell. 'His computer might help. Is it still working?'

'It's all in one piece,' said Garden.

Campbell went by himself up into Flagg's studio. The socket for the plug was at an awkward angle so he pulled out the computer desk. As he did so a piece of paper, which had been stuck down the back, fell to the ground. Bending down to pick it up he saw that it was an envelope. He decided to ask fingerprints to take a particular look at it. On lifting the flap and feeling inside he found a lock of dark hair folding in his gloved fingers. Forensics could check that too, he decided.

Having returned the envelope to the condition in which he found it he placed it in a plastic bag and sealed the opening. He leaned across and powered up the computer. He hated modern technology but like the car he hated to drive he could see it had to be mastered.

He loaded several documents in turn. The memory stick's outer casing was broken, but otherwise it was intact. They were entitled 'G Franson' and numbered. But they were protected in some way so he couldn't read their contents. This was frustrating. But was it frustrating enough for the person viewing them to smash everything in sight?

Campbell was now sure that Flagg had taken the memory stick from Geraldine's flat.

Over the years, Campbell had come to realise, he'd become his job. It wasn't just something he did to earn the money to keep his home and family. The attributes required to do the work had become his attributes also and, no doubt, the problems in his personality could be traced to the same reason. So he tried to see why Flagg had taken evidence.

Campbell remembered how his own drive to solve the problem of the body on Catstail Sandbank had made him get Garden and Jenner to bring information to him against Tarnish's wishes when he was ill in bed. He understood that drive for knowledge. But Campbell had not prevented anyone else from seeing the information as Flagg had done. Hiding knowledge, he thought, was a crime in itself. No progress could ever be made like that.

But was it Flagg who'd broken the memory stick? Flagg may have been behaving oddly by stopping people in their cars to get some power kick but was someone else involved in wrecking the place -- someone involved with the body on the sandbank?

He pulled out Geraldine's memory stick to see if its contents could be discovered back at the office. Putting it in an evidence bag, he went outside. By the garage he found a uniformed policeman and he checked with him that there would be an officer here at all times in case Flagg, or anyone else, returned.

Campbell drew up in the monastery yard and turned off his headlights. He was answering a phone call from Lara Elves. Even with her last tale not being validated by another witness he still had to investigate. After all, the story was consistent with her last one. She said she'd seen the people she'd seen before. The same ones that had dumped what she'd thought to be the body found on Catstail Sandbank. They were at the monastery today for a retreat. Campbell didn't believe Lara enough, however, to tie up any more of his officers. He was here on his own.

The light from a door bell glowed next to the second door along the monastery building. Having rung it and waited, Campbell was soon following the direction given by Brother Joshua's open hand into the hallway. He could hear a computer being worked in an office to his right but was taken into a living room on the left. He found himself surrounded by a square of blue flowered fabric chairs.

'I expect you want to know if Carroll Enderby came to the retreat today, Inspector?' asked Brother Joshua.

'I didn't know she'd planned to,' said Campbell deciding to put Lara's tale to one side while he could learn more of Carroll Enderby.

'She booked in one day last week at my suggestion. We were going to pray for Geraldine Franson. Have you found Carroll yet?'

'Sadly, no.' Campbell looked around the room noting the crumpled seats and cushions, and the pencils worn down to stubs. The conversation had brought him to where he wanted to be: he needed to check on Lara's latest story. So he asked, 'Are the people who came for the retreat still here?' he asked.

'They've all left now, Inspector. We had six today. We normally keep our numbers down to four.'

The emptiness of the monastery confirmed to Campbell that he was right to come alone.

'What is all this about, Inspector?' asked Brother Joshua.

'I would like all the names and addresses of those who came today,' said Campbell as he thought whether Lara Elves had been telling the truth about the retreat.

'May I ask why, Inspector?'

'You know I don't have to tell you, Brother Joshua. And right now I haven't the time to explain. What I need from you is co-operation – if such a thing exists in your credo?'

'I'm sorry, Inspector. Of course.' Brother Joshua went out of the room and returned moments later with the visitors' book.

The names meant nothing to Campbell as he put them down in his note book. None of the addresses were local. 'Did you know any of them personally?' he asked.

'No, Inspector, I didn't know any of them. I took the bookings about ten days ago. I assumed the people had seen one of our adverts in the religious papers. We don't run this place as a business but no-one would know we were here if we didn't say so.'

He'd heard enough from Brother Joshua, now Campbell felt he ought to see Lara Elves and ask her again about her story. It seemed strange that people from different parts of the country could have come to the fens, firstly to dump something in the river from a boat under the new bridge, and secondly to come on a retreat at this monastery. Either there was a connection between these people or Lara Elves was making it up. And he would find out the truth from her now.

So he asked for her and Brother Joshua said, 'As you wish, she's in the kitchen.' And the monk took him out into the corridor. The last time Campbell had visited the kitchen he'd been taken directly across the yard. This time he was taken through a door at the end of the entrance hall which took him into a corridor running to the right, directly behind the sitting room he'd just been in. He stopped at the end while Brother Joshua opened another door. Looking down at his feet he marvelled at the golden glow of the parquet flooring. No doubt, he thought, provided by Renie Blacking's polish.

The next moment Campbell was standing in the base of the look-out tower. He remembered the stairway going up from his first visit but this time he noticed a small door set into a pointed arch to the side. The height of the tower, he calculated would allow for a ground floor room and one above it before the look-out area. And he couldn't recall seeing another door off the stairway.

The far door beyond the stairs and out of the look-out tower was being held open by Brother Joshua. Campbell entered the kitchen and found it empty.

'She's probably with her babes,' said Brother Joshua. 'She's put them in my room.'

Beyond the kitchen, doors opened off another corridor. All the room doors were on one side with a row of windows on the other wall looking onto the yard like a cloister. Brother Joshua took the second door. The pale glow of a night light shone on tiny faces wrapped and tucked into a double bed.

'The bed is to accommodate my size,' apologised Brother Joshua. 'The children are taking a nap. That's where Lara puts them.'

But Campbell could see no Lara so Brother Joshua shut the door.

'Brother Michael keeps his door locked. His disability makes him feel insecure,' explained Brother Joshua nodding at the first door in the corridor.

Campbell watched Brother Joshua call at and try the end door which turned out to be an empty bathroom.

'Perhaps Brother Michael knows where she is,' said Campbell.

'He's in the back office. On the way I can try the chapel while you can go up to the look-out room,' suggested Brother Joshua.

'I'd like to look at both,' said Campbell.

'Of course,' agreed Brother Joshua.

Campbell entered the small chapel at the bottom of the look-out tower and found the room to be two stories high. At the top small slit windows on three sides told Campbell there was no room between the chapel and the look-out area. He could remember seeing them on the outside of the tower and one row of them on the inside along the stairway. In here, on one side, they let in shafts of moonlight into the chapel illuminating the single bench and kneeler in front of a tall statue of a saint in blue robes. It awakened a childhood memory for Campbell for a moment – a respect for religion imposed on him by his mother. The religious, as far as she was concerned held some secret knowledge of God that ordinary folk had no hope of knowing.

He blinked it away. Lara was going to be found. Geraldine, Carroll, Flagg. There would be no more missing people – he couldn't let there be. Campbell turned and left the chapel to take the stairs up the tower.

At the top a light shone in his eyes from the corner of the room. The beam fell with a clatter from a dropped torch. His eyes tried to recover from the dazzle. He thought he saw Geraldine Franson's face looking back at him highlighted by the upward arc of light. Logic told him it couldn't be so. Then he remembered Garden's talk of twins. Could it be? Blinking he looked again to see Carroll Enderby before him. He uttered her name.

The person in front of him hidden under a rug except for her face made a pained wail. Campbell shook his head; he knew he was looking at Lara Elves.

'I'm sorry,' she cried. 'I knew I'd done wrong as soon as I'd phoned you.'

Campbell crouched over her and pulled back the rug. 'I've found her,' he called to Brother Joshua. 'Stay there. I'll bring her down in a minute.' Then he turned to Lara and asked, 'Why did you make up such a story, Lara?'

'At first I wanted to be special – the story with the boat an' all. All I do is clean and cook, here or at home. Then today...'

'What about today, Mrs Elves?'

'You've got my mum and dad in prison,' said Lara. 'I know my dad would niver kill nobody. He niver killed Geraldine Franson. So I thought I could pull you away from him. Give you someone else to chase.'

'But you were asking me to suspect real people – the people who came to the retreat today. You could have got them into trouble.'

'I know. I know,' she wailed. 'But my mother and father have done nowt wrong.'

'Is that what they've told you?'

Lara shook her head, 'They hint told me nowt.'

'Lara, it looks as though your parents have been involved with people smuggling.' No matter how he tried to soften the words with his Edinburgh accent he knew they were harsh. But her face remained still. Campbell realised that she was too shocked to react. He didn't want to invade her privacy by touching her so he let her stand by herself and walked in front of her down the steps to Brother Joshua.

Lara must hate me, thought Curran Elves, to get herself into this much trouble with the police. He didn't want to face the police with the green gem so recently thrown away. He feared they could almost smell dishonesty.

As he got out of his old battered van he found himself in front of the Scottish Inspector. He heard Inspector Campbell thank him for coming so soon and then say that Lara was frightened. The Inspector's accent made Curran take a moment to work out what he'd said. But it struck him that she'd never been frightened in her life. She didn't know what fear was.

'Surely,' said Inspector Campbell, 'you can't make your money hand collecting shell fish in this day and age?'

Curran just stared at him. "What a stupid question to ask now." The wound of his wife's trouble with the police made him feel the Inspector was levering damaged flesh apart with this interrogation. Anger flared up to his tongue.

'I don't just collect shell fish though they fetch a reasonable price; I trawl for shrimps too. Sometimes the price for them is quite good too. But the fishing's so dropped off, I shall soon have to look for something else. We don't live well, Inspector. You can come and see my poor little home anytime you like. There are more things broken than I shall ever have enough money or time to fix.'

Curran started towards the kitchen door where he could see Brother Joshua waiting.

'Did you know,' asked Inspector Campbell, 'that Geraldine Franson and yourself are related?'

Curran stopped. The sight of the body on the sand bank came back to him like a vast wave hitting the side of his boat. 'No. In what way?' He stumbled over the words.

'Her grandmother, Georgina Brightwood, and your grandmother, Charlotte, were sisters. Charlotte told me herself.' Inspector Campbell stood between him and the kitchen door. 'Hawser was their maiden name.'

Curran shook his head. Perhaps Harry Blacking was right, perhaps it was a curse. If Geraldine Franson had been a cousin then she'd joined his family – mother, father and grandfather – in death out on the Wash. It fitted the pattern of disaster around him. He felt somehow to blame for their destruction.

'Does that make me a suspect?' he asked.

'I have no evidence that you knew her directly, though she knew your father-in-law, Harry Blacking, well enough.'

'I won't have nothing to do with him.'

'Won't you?'

'Harry Blacking killed my mother and father and grandfather, if that isn't enough for you...'

Curran could feel the heat of his reddening skin.

'Do you have any evidence that he killed your family?' asked Campbell.

'Not what you'd call evidence,' replied Curran. 'And what good is it knowing Geraldine Franson was a relative now she's dead? It's too late.'

'Some things we learn are not relevant,' said Inspector Campbell nodding in agreement with him. 'We have to discard them. You have to move a lot of soil when you dig a hole.'

Curran laughed. The Scotsman was mad.

'Your bairns are in here,' said Inspector Campbell who was already ahead of him. Curran followed him towards the kitchen until Campbell stopped and stood aside to let him in the door.

He ached to hold his children so he pushed past Brother Joshua saying, 'If Lara hadn't come to work here none of this would have happened.' All he knew was that he wanted to get them home and keep them all safe including his wife. 'And Lara?' he asked.

Curran packed his bundles of children onto the van floor surrounding them with cushions taken from the chairs in the monastery living room. Having shut the back door of the van, he came round to the front to find Brother Joshua lifting Lara wrapped in blankets into the front seat. He wanted to push the monk out of the way but found he was already moving back. Curran fitted the seat-belt around her. Yes, she was his and he would keep her warm and safe too.

Flagg hated the cold in his arms and legs. They were stiff. He ached. Sleeping in a car in November was hell.

"Monday stinking morning," he thought. Today he'd get Stranfield for giving him the wrong information. Carroll Enderby hadn't been out on the Wash – not at the access route by the monastery anyway. The monk in the wheel chair had told him. The two people he'd thought to be Carroll Enderby and Harry Blacking had been just bait diggers getting lugworm for rod and line fishermen. And Flagg couldn't wait there when he'd been seen by the monk. He'd lost endless time. He had to get Carroll Enderby. She knew about Geraldine Franson. And Stranfield would pay for his stupidity.

He swung open the driver's door and got out of his car. He pissed into the bracken in the woods. He couldn't have chosen a better place to wait, he told himself, so close to the laboratory.

Back driving, his car slipped and gripped the sandy track under him 'till he reached the road. Just round the bend found himself on the stretch of road where he'd stopped Carroll Enderby. The memory of the power he'd had over her for that brief time gave him immense pleasure.

At the laboratory car park he stopped and waited for Stranfield. At eight twenty-five he saw a car appear out of the woods at the top of the road. He watched it pass through the criss-cross of ditches and banks, getting larger with its increasing closeness. Flagg felt his muscles tighten.

The car stopped close to the laboratory door. A tall red-bearded man got out and stared at him. Flagg stared back.

On the phone Stranfield had sounded like a bull, and now Flagg saw that he walked like one as he came towards him.

Stranfield stepped closer and Flagg's biceps flexed. He stepped again and Flagg's fists curled. The red bull was waiting by Flagg's car door. Flagg's nerves sparked inside him. He knew he was ready to fight.

He flicked open the door wide just catching Stranfeield's arm. He stepped out of the car and punched Stranfield's face; heard the skin split; punched Stranfield's gut; saw Stranfield fold.

So Flagg went to punch Stranfield out. But his fist hit nothing. He felt his own head thrust back, pain in his cheek. Then there was pain in his gut. He gasped.

'Attack me, would you?' taunted Stranfield from above him. 'What for?'

The ground was hard. Gravel grated against his loins. Flagg felt Stanfield's hard leathered foot against his thigh. 'You told me Carroll Enderby was out on the mud flats with Harry Blacking,' wined Flagg.

'She was,' Stranfield insisted putting more weight behind his boot.

'She wasn't,' gasped Flagg. He wanted to hit this bull of a man so hard he couldn't talk. He straightened his legs, stooped his body slightly and thumped Stranfield as hard as he could.

The damaged face of the laboratory man staggered back from him. He surged forward. "Finish him. Finish him," he thought.

Flagg's jaw cracked. Stranfield must've hit him. Pain shot up through his skull. He could feel himself falling back onto the car park and then there was blackness.

The light hurt Flagg's eyes. And his jaw throbbed. Plastic tiled flooring chilled his back. Coarse rope scratched at his wrists and ankles. He pulled himself up and saw a small office waiting room. He guessed it belonged to the laboratory as he heard Stranfield say,

'Don't bother to speak. I've fixed your mouth shut with tape. You must be a madman. I don't know what life has done to you but there's no excuse for your actions.'

Flagg could see his own identity card being waved in front of him.

'You're a policeman,' said Stranfield. 'I thought you might not be a real policeman when you attacked me, but now I see you are.'

Flagg wanted to kill him. He snatched at his bindings.

'So why did you attack me? It couldn't possibly be over something as petty as my information, given in good faith, being wrong. So perhaps you thought in your youthful naivety that I had something to do with Geraldine's demise. Well, I can assure you, on that score, you are wrong. But that cow deserved all she got.'

Flagg leaned back against the fabric covered foam and metal frame of the chair seat behind him. The floor dug into his hips so he stretched out his bound legs and kicked the coffee table to one side. Stranfield pushed it with his foot back onto Flagg's legs.

'She took,' continued Stranfield, 'all the progress we'd made in the last six months. But I can't prove it because she didn't document any of it here. She's taken that information. And if I could find it I wouldn't need her anyway.'

Flagg liked Stranfield's internal discomfort. It softened his own. He liked Stranfield's swollen eye and fat, cut lip.

'There was nothing in her flat,' said Stranfield. 'I looked when she went on holiday.'

Flagg wanted to laugh: the idiot couldn't have looked very well. Stranfield wanted the computer records and he had them at his own home. And he couldn't tell him because his mouth was taped up.

'First,' went on Stranfield, 'I'm going to phone the press about you. And then the police can have you back.'

Flagg watched the door slam shut behind Stranfield. He fought against the pain in his jaw and his bindings until sirens – police and ambulance –

cut through the air from the edge of the woods.

Chapter 15

Campbell watched Tarnish's glowing pate as his superior officer spoke to him. 'They can't find Agatha Spier in West Africa,' said Tarnish.

Campbell regretted allowing Roger Rick the room to manoeuvre by holding back the jewel-swap scam from Tarnish. He should have known Roger Rick would not have let Agatha Spier talk to the police because of the chance of losing his money to the West African authorities. Campbell put this oversight down to leaving his sick bed too soon. And suddenly he felt that he'd behaved no better than Flagg keeping the computer records from Geraldine's flat.

'There's no doubt,' continued Tarnish, 'that you've done well to uncover the goings on at that Bed and Breakfast establishment, but we still have no-one charged for the murder of Geraldine Franson.'

Campbell found he could say nothing but, 'Yes, Sir,' as evenly as he could.

'So I want you to go back to Jack Wren in the hospital and interview him under caution. Get one of the tape-recorders set up. That man killed Geraldine Franson.'

Campbell started to explain that he'd like to pursue the connection between Harry Blacking and Geraldine Franson but Tarnish interrupted with,

'You won't need to once you've spoken to Jack Wren.'

Campbell watched Garden swing in and out of the traffic on their way to the hospital, her freckled face never looking from the task of driving.

'Did you,' he asked, 'check the register of births to see if Geraldine Franson had a twin?'

'There was nothing recorded,' said Garden, 'But Jack Wren might know if anything tricky went on.'

After his experience in the look-out tower with Lara Elves looking like

Geraldine Franson and Carroll Enderby he found himself nodding at the possibility of a twin.

In the hospital he thought Jack Wren looked completely unlike a murderer with his head of malted white hair tilted on one side innocently listening to his neighbour in the general ward. Campbell was delighted: a private room would have to be found for a formal interview so he didn't tell Garden to get the equipment from the car.

Jack Wren turned away from the conversation he was having and lifted his hand in greeting to Campbell. Again Campbell was stabbed by the guilt of bringing this man back into a life of grief and torment. But he pushed the thought away. It was clear the man's health and humour were improving and there was an outstanding question he had to ask him. After chatting with him for a few minutes Campbell dropped it into the conversation.

'Did Geraldine have any dental work done abroad?' With an answer of 'Yes,' the question of twins would retreat and he could allow the body on Catstail Sandbank to rest in peace.

'Not as far as I know,' said Jack Wren. 'She had good teeth. I can't remember her having anything major done to them. Why?'

'The body on Catstail Sandbank had dental work, crowns. One of the local dentists thought it could have been done abroad.'

'So my Geraldine might not be dead after all?'

Campbell could see the hope rising in the pale skin of the Canadian. He knew he felt the same himself, but it didn't take away the fact that a woman had died. And the hair was the same as Geraldine's, so now he had to ask if there was a twin sister.

As he opened his mouth to speak the ward doors swung open and Tarnish started to march towards Campbell. Jenner was scurrying behind him and slightly to one side so Campbell could see from her face that she was trying to warn him.

Having moved away from Jack Wren's bed Campbell reached Tarnish before he arrived within the hearing distance of the veteran airman. As Campbell led Tarnish back out of the ward his superior said,

'I told you, "formal interview under caution."'

'It wasn't practical,' said Campbell. 'And he says Geraldine didn't have any major dental work done, let alone foreign.'

'He lived in Canada. We have Geraldine's hair for heaven's sake. It matches the body.'

Campbell watched Tarnish tell Jenner to inform Jack Wren of his rights and caution him. Campbell felt a shout build up inside his chest. 'You're wrong,' he wanted to yell. But instead he turned away.

'Where are you going?' asked Tarnish.

'There will be a delay while Jack Wren gets a solicitor and a room is set up. I've things I can be doing while I wait.'

The constant dark of the bomb shelter unsettled Carroll Enderby. The sounds of people moving about above her during Sunday had kept her crouching silently on the bed. There'd been a period of quiet followed by some further movement later on. Then there'd been long hours with nothing to do except read the only book provided, the Bible. She couldn't touch it after Brother Michael's quotations. It had made her aloneness lonely. And she was trying to save the torch batteries. She didn't quite trust Brother Michael to bring her more because although he'd brought her food it had not been at regular times. The clock on the wall had told her that as well as her body.

A shaft of light broke into the bomb shelter and across her thoughts. She'd done a lot of thinking, worked things out. Now she would have it out with Brother Michael. She watched the food basket come down through the hatch on a piece of string. She went over to the steps.

'Brother Michael?'

'Yes,' he said. 'Don't come up. You're best where you are.' She noted the low tones in his local accent.

'Brother Michael?' she asked again, building her nerve.

'Yes.'

'Brother Joshua was the boyfriend Roger Rick said Geraldine had at university, wasn't he?'

'Yes, but you know that already.'

'Did he beat her, like Roger Rick said?'

'Brother Joshua told me that Geraldine used to drink heavily when she was a student. It made her eyes sensitive to light.'

'She found out where Joshua was,' Carroll continued. 'She wanted to contact her old college friend. She put the number down on the back of a note from Stranfield. But Joshua didn't answer the phone, you did. Like you did the time I phoned. You befriended her.'

There was silence from above.

Fear coursed through Carroll. Perhaps Brother Michael had killed Geraldine Franson and the bomb shelter had been her prison before her death. Brother Michael was not as feeble as he liked to make out.

She rushed up the steps. As she reached the hatchway the end of a pole smacked her across her crown followed by the metal window hook, which caught the back of her head. She fell back and tumbled down the stone steps. As she tried to make air come back into her lungs she heard him say,

'And shouting won't do you any good at all. Brother Joshua knows all about you and Geraldine. He's in on this. And there are no housekeepers around. Just think about that.'

The hatchway slammed and she heard a lock scratch shut. For several minutes Carroll had too little breath to think of anything.

Outside the interview room Campbell listened to DS Parnold, at last returned from the Met, saying, 'Harry Blacking's confessed to bringing in a man to live at the Bed and Breakfast place. He reckons he knows nothing about how the vacancy there was made.'

'It's not that I really want to talk to him about, if you don't mind me interrupting your interview?' asked Campbell.

Parnold smiled and opened the door. Campbell knew that Parnold would be pleased for his interviewee to be aggravated by extra questioning. It would weaken Harry Blacking's ability to lie.

While Parnold did the formalities Campbell looked at Harry Blacking's square lined face and thought he might just be ready to talk given the right questions. He thought he would ease his way in with one he and Harry both knew the answer to already. 'Did you bring in or take out of this country Geraldine Franson during the end of October or the beginning of November?'

'I told you, no, already.'

'So who did you bring in? And I don't mean for the Bed and Breakfast place either.' Campbell saw Harry Blacking look away. He'd registered a hit, so he continued, 'Was she small, about Geraldine's size?'

Harry's face froze.

'Harry?' asked Parnold.

'I didn't kill her,' said Harry Blacking.

'So who was she?' asked Campbell.

'They'll kill me, if I tell.'

'Who will kill you?' asked Campbell.

'They gave me so much money. That sort of money buys silence.'

'But I know already,' said Campbell, delighted that his guess had been right. The girl on Catstail sandbank had to have come from somewhere and Harry Blacking had to be the most likely source.

'You didn't bring her right in, did you?'

'I had instructions. They came in an envelope with the money. I was to drop her off on the mud flat that runs up to the sea bank near that cranky monastery. But she wasn't wearing a silken evening dress when I left her.'

'What was she wearing?' asked Campbell.

'Warm things: a balaclava, thick jacket and rubber boots. So it couldn't have been the dead girl. And I never saw her face prop'ly. And the dead girl had no face anyhow.'

'But,' said Campbell, 'you thought it was her when you saw the body on Catstail Sandbank?'

'I thought I'd sent the girl to her death letting her walk across the mud flats on her own. I thought the tide had swept her away and out to sea and then left her on the sandbank. I thought the black stuff flapping about her could have been her underwear or some of the black plastic bags that litter the sea.'

Campbell understood why Harry Blacking had not wanted to look at the body when they'd stood together on Catstail Sandbank. It had not been revulsion but fear that his face might show recognition. He asked him, 'When did you drop her off on the mud flat?'

'Seven in the morning, first of November,' Harry Blacking answered.

'Why didn't you say anything?'

'Because all the rest of my business would be found out. And then there was all that money I'd taken for the job. And when I saw the black silk was too long to be underwear and too fine to be plastic, I knew it wasn't her, or if it was she'd not met her fate because I'd left her on the mud flats with the tide about to turn.'

'So what did you think when Carroll Enderby ran from you across the mud flats on Saturday?'

'I thought, "My God, she's going to end up like that other one."'

'Could that other one have been Geraldine Franson?'

'I didn't get a real good look at her like. I didn't want to. I don't want to learn too much about these people. That's not my job. She was wrapped up against the cold. She was small like her, but I never thought about it because that int the way Geraldine carries on.' Harry Blacking thought for a moment as if some memory of the place was returning to him. 'And, anyway, I thought there was a boat pulled up on the sandbank. I couldn't see it proper like. It was in the shadows.'

Campbell leaned back in his chair allowing it to dig into his spine and watched Parnold ask Harry Blacking where he kept his money because there wasn't much in his bank account. Harry Blacking turned his eyes to the ceiling and Campbell got up to go.

Campbell came out of the interview room and found Garden waiting for him.

'Escaped the hospital then?' he asked her, thinking how Jack Wren must feel at being treated as a suspect for murder.

'Jenner's still there,' said Garden.

'Jack Wren has taken a turn for the worse. A minor heart attack so the doctors say.'

Campbell shook his head. He would not get the chance to ask the Canadian whether Geraldine was one of twins for a while yet. So he resorted to his internal shopping list of unfinished leads and asked Garden about the envelope of hair he'd found in Flagg's studio which he'd sent to fingerprints and forensics.

'For speed the envelope and the hair were split,' she said. 'I'll phone them and ask.'

As Garden's ponytail bobbed down the corridor Campbell felt the ghost of the dig in his spine from the interview room chair. It reminded him of another conversation he'd had. He too needed a phone.

Back in his office he found and dialled the number for Newington University. He asked if Professor Roger Rick was there and was told that he was lecturing at this moment in lecture theatre five and, if he wanted to, he could leave a message for the professor to phone him back.

So when Garden came into his office he said, 'Geraldine Franson is alive.'

'How do you know?' she asked.

'Because Roger Rick said if she was dead he would commit suicide. And I don't think he lied. The story of Geraldine's death has been in the paper since Saturday and today he is lecturing as usual at his university.'

'It might take him a while to bring himself to do it.'

'I don't think so. He's obsessed with her. And, I thought there'd have been an extradition order from West Africa for Roger Rick by now. You would think after what Tarnish told them they would have him back in a flash, unless they have no evidence. No Agatha Spier, no jewels, and no Geraldine Franson. After all, we haven't even got a formal statement from him. I think it's time to bring Roger Rick in. Can you arrange that with the local force for the University, Garden?'

'Yes Sir. But I think you might like to look at this.' She handed him a report. 'The hair in the envelope you found in his studio is Geraldine's and the envelope is covered in the same fingerprints as were found everywhere in her flat – we think they must be Geraldine's.'

'Don't looked so worried,' said Campbell. 'I don't think Flagg's murdered anyone, and certainly not Geraldine Franson.'

Garden asked, 'How do you know, sir?'

'There's been a report that he's been picked up at the laboratory and taken to hospital. The attending officers didn't recognise him at first with black hair. They thought he and Stranfield had been fighting. Stranfield was brought in to the police station but released. He said that nothing had happened and Flagg agreed, shortly before his jaw was wired up.'

'Fagg's broken his jaw?'

'Looks like it.'

'And Geraldine?'

'Separate issue.'


Carroll Enderby opened her eyes. Her back ached, but at least she'd managed to get herself back on the bed and from here she saw the hatchway open. For a moment no shadows cast across the beam of light and she waited for the basket of food to be lowered on its string. Instead, a pair of feet and ankles the same size as her own appeared.

The woman's silhouette came towards her. She couldn't see her arms or hands because she was holding them in front of her. Suddenly the story in Saturday's newspaper had to be wrong. Carroll knew Geraldine was not dead.

'Geraldine?' she called out.

'Yes, Carroll.'

'I'm so pleased you're alive.' Carroll struggled to sit up. The aches from her fall down the steps were easing. 'Are you a prisoner too?'

'You care too much about me.' Geraldine stopped halfway between the steps and Carroll's bed.

'The world thinks you're dead,' said Carroll.

'Well, I'm not. And I wouldn't be here if it wasn't for you.'

'I've been looking for you.'

'I know,' said Geraldine.

Carroll saw Geraldine's shadowed hands move and the light from the hatchway caught something bright she was holding.

'Do you know where I got this?' Geraldine moved so Carroll saw the blade. 'A cauliflower field. They'd used it for cutting off the root and outer leaves.'

'You did take information about the chip,' said Carroll. Fear flicked through her as the knife swished passed.

'Of course I took the chip and I left the files in a mess so you would get into trouble. I wanted you sacked. You were always nosing into everything. You thought I didn't know you'd been through my desk. Well you were wrong.'

'You don't have to kill me. I don't know anything.'

'No-one else will kill you. That's why I'm here. You made the connection between me and the monastery.'

'You left the telephone number on the back of a note from Stranfield. You must have dropped it.'

'Stranfield was going to get rid of me. He said I was too greedy. He said I couldn't have half shares in the patent. The investors had to get something back for the money they'd laid out. He didn't like my alternative idea. It was my brain that was being used. My knowledge, my intelligence.'

'So you were going to take everything?'

'Yes, I've taken it all. There was the data I collected doing my own work and then I had to find the data Stranfield had hidden. He had slipped it into the paper files. The smallest of data chips placed here and there. The man thought they would be safe from computer hackers.'

Carroll thought about the jumbled files. It all made sense. Nearly every office she'd ever worked had kept their records on computer.

'And I now have enough money to develop this chip myself,' continued Geraldine. 'Brother Michael will get some local fisherman to get me the fresh shell-fish in a couple of months. And do you know this little monastery is a real haven for electronics experts. Knowledge is power and power is money. Everyone was happy to think of me as dead except you, little sister.'

'Don't call me little sister,' said Carroll. 'I'm not your sister.'

'I'd kill you now except we don't want to mess up this nice little hidey hole. When the tide's right I'll take you down on the mud flats.'

The hospital corridor echoed Campbell's footsteps around him. Garden had gone to see how Jenner was fairing with Tarnish and Jack Wren. Flagg, Campbell noted, had been allocated a room on his own and a constable to guard him. He felt there must have been some hiccup in the system to allow Flagg's tendencies to go undetected until they spilled out into his recent strange behaviour.

'His jaw's wired up,' explained the constable. 'He can't talk properly.'

'Thank you,' said Campbell, going through the door. 'I did hear about it..' He was prepared: he got out a note book out. Flagg would have to write his answers down.

The black hair of his former colleague against the white of the pillow caused Campbell to look again at the man in the bed. Green eyes flashed back at him out of a bruised face.

'So much hate,' said Campbell. 'Why?' He offered his pencil and paper to Flagg.

"Renie Blacking," wrote Flagg.

'I sent you to check on Harry Blacking and you called on Renie, then I went round to see Renie? I don't think so. You were going around in a mock police car before that.'

"Policing without pay," wrote Flagg.

'No,' said Campbell, 'you cannot police without permission.'

Flagg snatched back the pencil and paper and wrote, "I had to know more than you."

Reading it Campbell thought that this was not what he'd come to see Flagg about, so he asked him, 'Where did you get the envelope with the hair we found in your house?'

"Geraldine Franson's flat," wrote Flagg, "useless love token." And he gouged the pencil into the paper.

Campbell took the notebook from him and turned the page.

'I know you had a fight with Stranfield.' He passed him the paper.

"No fight," wrote Flagg. "Stranfield gave false information about Carroll Enderby's location."

'Did you find Carroll Enderby?'

Flagg wrote, "No."

'Where did you look?'

"On the mud flats by the monastery. Stranfield sent me. She wasn't there."

'When?'

"Saturday am."

'She was there. She went out with Harry Blacking. There's a witness to that.'

"Cripple monk said bait diggers," wrote Flagg.

Campbell folded up his notebook. Brother Joshua had lied. He'd said Brother Michael and he had been in prayers all morning. And Flagg's story tied in with Lara's tale of the dark car and black haired man stopping in the lane by the monastery. There was no doubt in his mind that, at least on this, she'd told the truth.

'Thank you,' he said to Flagg.

Flagg lunged across at him and Campbell dodged back to avoid his clawing hands. He realised thanking Flagg had only emphasised the fact that Flagg had given his superior officer useful information.

'Knowledge kept to yourself is not a power over someone else,' said Campbell. 'It has to be seen in context with all the other pieces of information to have any power at all.'

As Campbell went out of the door he saw Flagg pull a lump of hair from his head so he asked the constable there to call a doctor.

Campbell found Jenner by her car, both of them discoloured by the yellow street lights in the hospital car park. She was loading the tape-recorder into the boot. It was getting late. He checked his watch, eight o'clock.

'They needed the room for patients,' Jenner explained. 'The interview with Jack Wren is off for now, you know?'

Campbell nodded as Garden barged through the swing doors at the front of the hospital.

'Do you remember,' asked Garden, 'those papers you got off Derek Browme, the newspaper man? Well, I've been on the phone to the office. I got them to run a check on the companies investing in Stranfield's laboratory. And on one of them, Joshua Alexander, is the main man.'

'I think,' said Campbell, 'despite the late hour a visit to the good Brothers is in order.'

Carroll Enderby thought the cold black wind was trying to swallow her up. She refused to care about the wrench on her scalp from Geraldine dragging at her hair to make her walk. She wasn't going to help Geraldine kill her by taking herself willingly to her death site. Her hands, bound behind her back, pulled on her shoulders. Her knees were bruised from their impacts with the wooden boarded path to the mud flats.

On reaching the top of the new sea wall Geraldine kicked Carroll's legs away from her. And with the pain Carroll remembered how fit Geraldine must have become with walking out on the mud flats regularly.

'You will have to wait or kill me here,' said Carroll hoping to delay Geraldine from her task. When they'd left the monastery Carroll had not seen or heard anybody and her yell for help had ended with a slap from Geraldine. But she had to hope, and pray. Because no-one would be able to find them if they went too far out there on the mud flats in the dark with the wind gathering up all sound and turning it into its own howling scream.

Chapter 16

Carroll rolled over on the sea bank and sat up. Her resistance, she knew, had drained Geraldine. The push from her former colleague, now that she thought about it again, was not from super fitness but to allow Geraldine herself to catch her breath. Her captor stood next to her and regained her grip on Carroll's hair.

'Tide's not down far enough yet,' said Geraldine. 'If we were by the river it would be best to dump you in while the tide is high but running out, but here I can kill you out on the mud while the tide is out and wait for the water to come and take you away.'

"Delay," thought Carroll, "I have to delay her." So she asked, 'Where did you go? You didn't fly to Spain like you said.' She was relieved that her fear had even got past the stage of affecting her voice with its usual crack. She'd somehow come through that into an area of her mind which was dead calm.

'When I went on holiday?' asked Geraldine. 'I went to and came back from Canada via Europe on the ferries. Transferred Grandfather's ticket to me. Mother went to Africa with the fake jewels.'

Carroll wanted to ask about Geraldine's grandfather and most of all: what fake jewels? But she thought it best to let Geraldine talk for as long as she liked.

'Mum was one gem short. My fault, I dropped it. But it didn't matter in the end. We've now got all the money we need. And Roger Rick won't be a problem.'

'Roger Rick?' asked Carroll.

'Shut up,' said Geraldine.

Carroll felt Geraldine's hand twist her hair.

As Campbell was driven into the monastery yard by Garden, Jenner said, 'Look, there's Brother Joshua.'

The headlights cut across the beam from another car. Campbell could see Brother Joshua standing on the ramp to the kitchen door with sagging bags of groceries. The light on the car roof which was leaving the monk, and now the yard, bore the sign, "TAXI".

When Campbell joined him with Garden and Jenner close behind, Brother Joshua said, 'Renie used to do our shopping.'

'You're late,' said Campbell.

'Time means little to me. I had to wait for a taxi,' said Brother Joshua. 'Such anxious faces?'

'I understand you are an investor in Stranfield's laboratory – where Geraldine worked?' queried Campbell.

'Yes, Inspector. Does that surprise you? Come in to the kitchen. It's warmer in here.'

Once inside Campbell sat at the table while Garden and Jenner stood to one side and Brother Joshua drew the curtains.

'You didn't say that you were involved in the laboratory,' said Campbell.

'Should I have? It didn't seem important, I have yet to make money on the investment. The whole thing was handled for me through investment brokers. I had no direct dealings with anyone there.' Brother Joshua put butter and yoghurt in the fridge from one of his grocery bags.

'Your monastery is very well equipped. It must have cost a fair bit to set this place up.'

'Inspector, before I became a monk I earned good money. Brother Michael and myself worked in ground breaking technology. I own the rights to several patents already.' Brother Joshua put cans in a cupboard while he spoke.

'Would you like,' asked Campbell, 'the sole rights to the work at Stranfield's laboratory?'

Campbell watched Brother Joshua come over and sit next to him. The monk's largeness made his soft actions seem to Campbell even gentler than they were.

'No, Inspector,' said Brother Joshua. 'I've retired from greed. I have more than enough to live modestly on here. I like to have a small involvement in science. It is part of my make-up. God has created such a fascinating world for us to discover.'

Campbell could find nothing incongruous in his answers so moved on to the incident on Saturday. 'I believe you lied to us, Brother Joshua,' he said.

'I have sinned,' agreed Brother Joshua. 'It seemed such a little lie, but it has been burning my conscience ever since. I even had the opportunity when you came to see Lara on Sunday to tell you the truth, but to be honest I haven't been myself, on and off, over the last couple of days.'

'Brother Michael was not in prayers on Saturday morning, was he?'

'Not the whole morning, like I said. He asked me to say that to you. I've become so used to protecting him. He said he thought he'd heard an intruder. He doesn't like people to know how nervous he is. When he came back he said no-one was there. I had no reason to disbelieve him. I hadn't heard anything myself.'

'And what about Lara's story about the car and the black haired man?'

'You know Lara, Inspector, she's full of stories.' Brother Joshua rose from the table. 'I'm sorry, Inspector. Brother Michael's usually in the back office at this time, perhaps we could go and see him.'

Campbell nodded.

'Inside or outside route?' asked Brother Joshua.

'Inside will be warmer,' said Campbell thinking of his recent illness.

The wooden corridor floors took them round to the front office door, which opened to reveal to Campbell that the back office door beyond was also open. The small computer room was empty. But Joshua stepped in calling for Brother Michael anyway.

'He can't be far,' said the big monk.

Campbell had to breathe in to let Jenner squeeze past into the back office, and Garden stayed by the front office door and kept watch on the corridor.

'I wanted to be like you,' said Carroll. 'I wanted to be respected.'

'You've been so easy to manipulate,' said Geraldine. 'You wanted a friend and you admired money.'

'Sitting in that cellar allowed me time to think. I forgot that you only get respect if you respect yourself.' Carroll felt a sharp twist of her hair.

And Geraldine smiled down at her. 'You had victim written all over you, right down to your speech impediment. Each life is the responsibility of its owner.'

'What about other people's lives, have you no responsibility for them?'

'Why should I?'

Carroll went for the question that had been burning at her since she realised Geraldine was alive: 'Did you kill the girl on the sand bank?'

'Of course I did. I don't need anyone else to do my killing. Are you stupid? The body was meant to be taken to be me. I could so easily become someone else and carry on without Stranfield. Only you wouldn't believe it.'

'Was that really the only way?' asked Carroll. This woman, who'd been her hero for so long, was completely insane. Reason could no longer reach her.

Campbell noted the blind at the front office window, with its rosary cord, was shut.

'Sir.' It was Jenner's voice from the back office.

It was his turn to squeeze back into the room past Brother Joshua and Garden. He gazed in the direction Jenner was pointing. On top of a pile of papers on the top shelf above some electronic equipment was a small pewter box – the size and shape of Charlotte's.

'The twin to Charlotte's box,' said Jenner.

'One of a pair,' corrected Campbell lifting it down. He examined the fishermen and birds moulded forever in action. The images were slightly different to Charlotte's box, but of similar design. He had to consider that this might well be the box given to Charlotte's sister and Geraldine's grandmother, Georgina Brightwood. The most likely person to have the box would be Geraldine's mother, Agatha Spier, so he asked Brother Joshua, 'Has Agatha Spier ever been here?'

'Geraldine's mother?'

'Yes.'

'No, I never met her, even when I was at college with Geraldine.'

'What about Geraldine?'

'No, Inspector. The box is Brother Michael's.'

Campbell put the pewter box down on a pile of papers and said, 'Flagg had all the information he needed. He just couldn't see that he had. Garden, have a look through these papers.'

The whir of an electric motor outside the window caught Campbell's attention. But Brother Joshua and then Jenner were nearer to the front door of the office and were outside before him.

The sound of the wheelchair was heading towards the old sea bank.

'I may,' said Carroll, 'not seem so bold as you. But I've had to fight to survive in my life. It has worn down my resistance. You've been pampered and spoilt.' She knew it was the wrong thing to say, but it didn't seem to matter anymore.

Geraldine screamed angrily in reply and yanked Carroll's hair. 'I've had enough of waiting. I just won't be able to take you out so far onto the mud flats. But the tide will still have taken you by morning.'

Campbell reached into his coat pocket for a torch and shone it on Brother Joshua. The big monk stood in front of the electric wheel chair which Brother Michael continued to run at him until Joshua went for the switch on the arm of the chair. There was a tussle between them. The heavy motorised chair tipped and the two monks tumbled down the old sea wall wrestling each other. The wheelchair was sliding down the wooden ramping on its side. The fever dream came back to Campbell. He'd seen this before – the exact patterns of their bodies. He rushed forward to separate them.

'It's him,' said Brother Joshua.

'He didn't kill Geraldine, Brother Joshua,' said Campbell levering at the big man's shoulder.

'He made me lie for him.'

'Geraldine's not dead,' said Campbell.

'I love her,' said Brother Michael.

'She made you love her,' said Brother Joshua. 'That's the way she works.'

'Where is she?' asked Campbell.

Brother Michael pointed along the walkway towards the mud flats.

Looking behind him Campbell saw Garden had come out of the office so he asked her to wait with the monks to make sure they didn't fight again.

'She's got Carroll Enderby,' said Brother Michael weakly.

Even though Campbell's illness had sapped his fitness he found himself running after Jenner towards the mud flats. Their feet rattled on the wooden boarding, but it was nearly a quarter of a mile to the new sea bank.

Carroll's captor had stopped. Carroll had resisted travelling far onto the mud flats and she could hear Geraldine panting. But she knew just a flick of Geraldine's knife would mean death.

Geraldine's grip on her hair shifted and she realised Geraldine was raising her knife hand ready to strike. So Carroll screamed loud and hard. Not for help, she didn't expect any. She had to distract her. It worked. Geraldine's grip on her hair loosened. Carroll pulled back, losing some strands to Geraldine's fingers, and she head-butted her in the stomach.

Geraldine fell back into the wet heavy mud. Carroll fell on top of Geraldine's knife arm and levered her fingers from the handle and took possession of the blade. She stopped.

Mixed in with the howl of the wind was a woman's shout. She was shouting Carroll's name. And when Carroll looked towards land she could see the small light of a torch.

'Here,' she screamed back. She hadn't the strength to bring Geraldine across the mud by herself.

'OK. Keep shouting,' said the voice.


'We'll wait here,' said Campbell, 'for assistance.' He sat on the new sea bank next to Geraldine who was handcuffed and in Jenner's firm grip.

'You knew I was alive,' said Geraldine.

'I'd become enticed by your shadow,' reflected Campbell.

'What did I leave behind that told you I was not dead?'

'An envelope of hair.'

'Just that?'

'My colleague thought it was a love token. But it wasn't your hair, was it? We were supposed to think it was. You'd obtained a sample of hair from the girl you were having brought over here and wrapped it into a hair brush newly bought for the exercise. We were meant to think she was you.'

Geraldine looked down. 'I smashed her jaw with the knife handle because she kept screaming. I couldn't look at her while I did it so I left her balaclava on. Then I undressed her and put her in my evening dress. I have to say, I hoped Stranfield would be blamed.'

'She was still alive when you left her,' said Campbell. 'She was breathing. She drowned.'

'I hoped the sea would make her unrecognisable.'

Campbell noted her coolness and asked, 'Where did she come from?'

'I don't know. There are plenty of people who want to live in this country. They will pay a fortune for it.'

'Indeed,' said Campbell. She appalled him.

Chapter 17

There had been no doubt in Campbell's mind that Geraldine would be locked up until her trial for murdering the woman who'd become the body on Catstail Sandbank. So it was without emotion that he drove from the court house to the hospital to pick up Jack Wren.

Having parked in the hospital car park he made his way into the foyer. As he walked towards the first of the maze of corridors he needed to take to get to Jack Wren's ward he was met by Lara Elves and her husband. Wrapped in Curran's arms was a bundle of life. As Campbell was offered a view of the baby girl he tilted his body over them and peeped at the infant's face. He was stunned to find that, tiny as she was, she was the image of her mother. He looked at the parents and found their faces alight with joy and love for each other and the child. Campbell smiled, at least the events of the last few weeks were behind them. For him, they would go on for months.

Following Geraldine's confession Campbell no longer needed to know from Jack Wren whether she had a twin, but he'd asked him anyway. Jack Wren hadn't known of any. But Campbell was delighted to be here, having locked the policeman part of him away for the afternoon. He was at the hospital as a friend to take Jack Wren to the airport. He already had his bags from Agatha Spier's house in the boot of his car. All there was to collect was the few things Jack Wren had in hospital and the man himself.

Campbell understood that Jack Wren didn't want to stay to support Geraldine. He said he wanted to go back to his life in Canada which, he now realised, was more real than the family he thought he'd had over here.

As Campbell took Jack Wren's small bag from the bed he heard him say, 'I haven't really thanked you.'

'I hardly returned you to an easy life,' said Campbell.

'No life is easy. You stopped me leaving it because of Georgina Brightwood's tinkering with facts. I don't see that as a just cause for taking my own life. That would have been letting her win.'

On returning to his office Campbell found Garden waiting at his door.

'There was nothing much on those computer records of Geraldine's we took from Flagg's house,' she said. 'Everything about the chip was on Brother Michael's computer.'

'I don't suppose she would've left the important stuff just lying around.'

'And,' said Garden.

Campbell noted a degree of irritation in her voice and decided she'd considered his last statement an insult, so he told her, 'Even if some things seem obvious we still have to check them out.'

'Sir?'

'What is it, Garden?'

'Agatha Spier's back from her trip. She went to Canada from Africa. The Canadian's chucked her out. She's down in the interview room with DS Parnold.'

'Ah, good,' said Campbell feeling his Scottish blood rising. He hoped Agatha Spier and Roger Rick could be charged with conspiracy to murder.

Campbell stood in a corner and listened to Parnold interviewing Agatha Spier. He seemed slicker and more at ease with his job since coming back from the Met. And Agatha Spier looked less like her photograph in Geraldine's flat with her grey hair un-tinted and collapsed against her tanned skin.

But it was clear to Campbell that she knew nothing of the murdered girl on the sand bank. She and her daughter were just transferring funds for Roger Rick as far as Agatha was concerned. Campbell was about to leave when she stopped and looked at him.

'Was it you who arrested my daughter?' she asked Campbell.

'Yes, Mrs Spier,' he replied.

'I can hardly believe she could do such a thing. She was spiteful as a child. She used to enjoy getting others into trouble, but I thought she would grow out of it.'

Campbell said nothing.

'I had another child you know. Geraldine had a sister. Mr Spier wasn't English, you know. He changed his name when he came over here to live. In his country if a couple are childless it is not uncommon for a brother or sister to give the couple one of their children. I gave them Geraldine's sister. My husband said it was enough to bring up one baby. You see they were twins. And now I feel I have lost Geraldine. I got a letter some time ago from my husband's brother saying how fascinated his girl had become with England. So much so she wanted to live over here. I shall try and contact her now.'

'What was her name?' asked Campbell.

'Rachel. It's funny, Inspector, Geraldine always wanted a sister.'

Campbell left the interview room to reread the forensic report about the hair. He'd focused on the hair on the brush. He'd seen through Geraldine's trick because of it. When he'd checked in the report later and found that the victim's hair had been elsewhere in the flat, not just in the hairbrush, he'd assumed Geraldine had been more subtle than he'd imagined.

He found Mary Brown, the scientist in charge of the forensics laboratory, only too happy to discuss her findings.

'Yes,' she agreed with him. 'It was most unlikely that all the hairs were planted. From the thin layer of dust we found it was clear Geraldine had cleaned up before leaving, but it would have been nearly impossible for her to clear up every single one of her own hairs.'

'Can I send you down some hair to compare with those you have already; just to be sure?'

'Yes, of course.' Mary Brown frowned. 'I heard you were ill.'

'Thank you for your concern. I was but I'm on the mend now.' And he knew the testing of Geraldine's own hair would only show that she'd killed her sister.

He wondered if that knowledge would at last reach inside Geraldine and pluck out remorse. Considering what her mother had told him he thought it would destroy her.

With a strange feeling of reaching his destination he said, 'If I'd read the report properly the first time I too would have assumed Geraldine to be dead. Because I was ill I only read part of it, so I carried on and came to the right conclusion using the wrong information. Sometimes you can know too much.' And he stretched his neck. He could lay the body on Catstail Sandbank to rest now he knew who she was.

Carroll Enderby looked out at the Wash. For the last time, she thought. She had nothing to stay here for. She allowed the wind to buffet her body as she stood on the new sea wall. The high tide covered most of the mud flats making the area she'd struggled over with Geraldine into a glistening green sea. A rustle behind her made her turn round to see Brother Joshua mounting the bank with his giant strides.

'I saw you come out here,' he said as he reached her, 'And I had to tell you that I didn't know Michael was keeping you in the bomb shelter. Brother Michael was drugging me with his sleeping pills. He told me before he went away with the police.'

'I guessed that.'

'Are you going to stay?'

'Don't worry about me Brother Joshua. I won't do anything dishonest again. Though Inspector Campbell says I didn't pass on to Derek Browme any more information about Stranfield's lab than was already on public records.'

'You don't have a job,' said Brother Joshua.

'I'm not religious, but I'll manage.'

'I'm not asking you to join a convent. I have connections in the scientific community. I can put you in touch with people – away from here.'

Carroll was too distracted to register his offer. 'There's one thing been eating at me. Stranfield told Geraldine to "leave something alone"?' she said. 'It clearly wasn't your old relationship with Geraldine. And I don't think he knew about Michael, so what could it have been?'

'Geraldine thought with a little tweaking the chip could be key in weapon development. Stranfield knew the dangers of that happening from the start that's why he'd set up on his own and got private investors.'

'How do you know that?'

'I'm one of the private investors.'

'I still can't like Stranfield,' said Carroll. 'So that was Geraldine's alternative idea. She told me he wouldn't accept it. He'll need a new scientist now there's no Geraldine.'

Joshua smiled. 'I have some talents in that area myself.'

Carroll smiled back. She realised her lack of gratitude for his offer of helping her find work. 'Thanks,' she said. 'We can talk about jobs on the way back to the car.' After all, she decided, a girl still had to make a living.

The End

# OTHER TITLES BY THIS AUTHOR

SMOKE SHADOWS (Inspector Campbell Mystery No 1)
by Pamela St Abbs  paperback and e-book


WATER WEAL (Inspector Campbell Mystery No 2)
by Pamela St Abbs  paperback and kindle e-book


THREADS OF TREASON by Mary Bale paperback and e-book
published by Pen and Sword, also in large print hard back

# ABOUT THE AUTHOR

Pamela St Abbs lived in Norfolk for most of her life.
She now lives in Scotland with her husband.

www.ingramcontent.com/pod-product-compliance
Lightning Source LLC
Chambersburg PA
CBHW060424130626
46555CB00005B/2208